Sophia's Version

by
Jane Biran

Strategic Book Publishing
New York, NewYork

Strategic Book Publishing
An imprint of AEG Publishing Group
845 Third Avenue, 6th Floor – 6016
New York, NY 10022
www.eloquentbooks.com

ISBN: 978-1-60693-718-1   1-60693-718-9

Printed in the United States of America

Cover Design: Peggy Ann Rupp, *www.netdbs.com*

Book Design: D. Johnson, Dedicated Business Solutions, Inc.

Dedicated to the memory of my brother
August 27, 1948–July 18, 2007

Footfalls echo in the memory
Down the passage which we did not take
Towards the door we never opened
—T.S. Eliot, from his poem *East Coker*

I owe a huge debt of gratitude to my husband, Yoav Biran,

who pushed me to publish my interminable writing

and believed I would succeed.

My great friend, Rosemary Ellerbeck [the author, Nicola Thorne]

likewise encouraged me.

Devorah Toft, who typed the manuscript had confidence that others would want to read it.

I should like to thank all at AEG Publishing Group and their colleagues at Strategic Book Publishing who proved that this faith in me was not entirely misplaced.

Jane Biran

Part One:
London, October, 1998,
The Family Funeral

Chapter One

"Don't you think we ought to tell our father that Mum has died?"

Michaela Rosen Clifton glared at her older sister. "What for? He didn't give a toss about her when she was alive. Why should he care now?"

"I think you're unfair to him," Sophia Rosen Schwartz replied. "He cared about her a lot more than you've ever given him credit for."

"You always were on his side. I suppose you'll tell him anyway in one of your loving daughter letters."

A look passed between the other two sisters that clearly said, "Here we go again," while their brother looked out of the window and wished he was somewhere else.

"Actually, if you don't mind my saying so, Michaela, I don't think you should use language like that when we are in a hearse." Esther Rosen Bloomfield had spoken in a voice so quiet she might have intended no one to hear her.

Michaela managed a smile of incredulity as she turned to Esther, the youngest of the four sisters.

"What language, sweetheart, are you referring to?"

"Toss," Esther suggested. "It's rude isn't it?"

This time they all laughed, even Sean, who was the most affected by the occasion that had drawn them together. Esther always had this effect on them.

"I don't think it is rude, as you call it, but it's not exactly kind either. And by the way, it is our mother who's in a hearse, not us. We're just in a car that follows the hearse."

1

"Does it have a special name?" This question was posed by Miranda Rosen Dickenson.

In her younger years, she was the sister referred to by the others as "the sandwich." This had been replaced later by "our rich sister."

"I think it is called a cortège," Sean Rosen said with a sigh. "But I actually don't think it matters all that much."

"No wonder you didn't pass your English exam my boy," snapped Michaela. "*We* are the cortège, not the bloody vehicle. The cortège is the procession, the people, not the cars."

"Michaela," stop being so aggressive," Sophia replied sharply. "It's really not appropriate considering why we're here and where we're going."

"Hear, hear," said Sean.

"You started it," Michaela retorted, "by bringing up the question of should we tell Mr. X."

"I wish you wouldn't call him that," Esther pleaded in her small voice. "He is Mum's ex-husband, but he is not our ex-father. No matter what you think of him, he will always be our father."

"Worse luck," sighed Michaela.

The others decided to drop the issue.

The five siblings were on the way to a crematorium in a place which, for reasons only Miranda claimed to understand, had been specified by their mother, Miriam Stern Rosen Katz, as part of her dying wishes. This extraordinary, but by no means uncharacteristic request by their mother had been the subject of a heated discussion between the siblings. Nevertheless, they agreed that her wishes should be respected. No one in the family had ever been cremated. Indeed, since the family was nominally Jewish, it had been considered a *goyische* thing to do. But since it was Miriam who had introduced the "nominally" into the family practices, none of her children could claim to be entirely surprised.

Sophia had pronounced cremation disconcerting. Esther had tentatively protested that the location was inconvenient and that she did not want her boys being witness to strange customs. Michaela had told her to shut up and stop being a Jewish mother. Miranda found her mother's choice of dispach to the afterlife not only acceptable but understandable in view of her lifelong unconventionality. Then they all noticed that Sean was crying. Michaela told him to stop being "a big girl's blouse," and the other sisters told her to shut up, which brought her to tears.

None of them could remember the last time they had seen Michaela cry.

"You've always picked on me," she said, "even when we were children.

Don't you understand that I am very upset? I was the closest to Mum.

I was the one she confided in. We have the same birthday. I was the most like her. She loved me the most."

"Possibly," Sophia responded, which was enough of a concession for Michaela's tears to dry up.

Sean appeared to start what promised to be a protest but then withdrew, and the others had fallen silent.

It was this discussion that each of them was now thinking about. Sophia, the eldest, had travelled the farthest to attend her mother's funeral. Long ago, she had stopped trying to fathom how her mother's mind worked. Mother and daughter had been a mystery to one another since the day Sophia had been born. And, as the years progressed, the gap in understanding had only grown deeper.

Sophia had left home when she started the university and had never returned. But she was a dutiful woman and had remained in regular touch. She had been available during times of crisis, which included Miriam's two divorces, and had provided uncomplaining financial support in the difficult periods that followed. She had slightly, and only infrequently, allowed herself to be bothered by her mother's expectations and the lack of acknowledgment for the help received.

Sophia could find plenty of excuses for her mother. Miriam had not had an easy life. Their father had certainly been more adept at begetting children than supporting them. In

Miriam's defence, she had been too spoiled in her own up-bringing to cope well with the economic uncertainties of being married to an actor.

But after her divorce, Miriam made the same mistake again. Only this time, it did not take twenty-four years before she realized her error. Michael Katz was a rather better and more fully employed actor than Eli Rosen, but he was also a womanizer and a spendthrift. In the interest of divesting herself of each of her husbands, Miriam conceded any alimony payments. As Michael Katz went out of the door, filial contributions came in.

Sophia sighed as she remembered her mother's letters. She never actually asked for anything but her needs were clear, and Sophia was never one to let her mother down. If closeness was measured by financial assistance, Sophia, not Michaela, would be the winner. But emotionally, Sophia suffered from lifelong guilt about her mother. The truth of the matter was that she had always loved her Aunt Rosa, Miriam's sister, more than her mother. She had been infinitely more devastated by Rosa's death than she could claim to be en route to her mother's funeral. She understood the reasons why, but it still felt wrong.

All the siblings had contributed to the payment of this funeral. Although she had pronounced cremation "disconcerting" to her siblings, which was the most tactful thing she could think of to say, Sophia privately thought it ludicrous. Cremation? If that was the way her mother wanted to go, fine. But why, in God's name, did it have to be in Chichester? They had never lived anywhere near Chichester. Neither their father nor Michael, as far as she knew, had ever appeared at the Chichester Theatre. And it was miles from where any of them lived and worked. Perhaps Miriam had seen the place and fancied it as an appropriate setting for her ashes. Perhaps all would be revealed when they arrived there.

Miriam's other sister, Alicia, and sundry friends, including some from the theatrical fraternity, were apparently making their own way to the crematorium. The siblings brought their mother's coffin from Highgate in a convoy of two cars—the hearse and the car they were in. Sophia had feared that their car would proceed at funereal pace from Highgate and was relieved to learn that after the first mile, hearses were permitted to speed up. "Our mother is in a flying coffin," Miranda had remarked, an apparent reference to Monty Python, a British television series that Sophia, who lived in California, had missed out on.

It was years since they had all been together. Even when Sophia had given a farewell party on the occasion of her departure with the love of her life for San Francisco, she had not managed to get them all together. Michaela and Miranda had not been on speaking terms at the time, so she invited Michaela and her brood to a separate dinner. When Michaela's elder daughter got married, the sisters had made up and were once again "communicado." However, she had not been able to attend. It had taken the death of their mother for a reunion to take place.

She looked from one to the other of her siblings wondering what thoughts were going through their minds. Sean, who was sitting next to her, was still looking out of the window. Esther, on her other side, kept looking at her mobile phone, anxious, as always, in case her boys were trying to reach her. The two warring sisters, Michaela and Miranda, had nobly volunteered to travel in the seats with their backs to the driver. Michaela was either asleep or, perhaps, pretending to be. Miranda was chewing gum and trying not to look at anyone.

They were a handsome lot, Sophia told herself. She, Sean, and Esther took after their father. Miranda and Michaela were spitting images of Miriam. Michaela was the best looking with her pretty hair and the tallest of the girls by several inches. All the siblings, except Sean and Sophia, tended to be overweight. They all had almond shape eyes of different shades of dark under thick, brown eyebrows. While they had all been dark-haired children the texture of their hair varied. . Sophia and Esther had straight hair, Michaela's was wavy,

and Miranda and Sean had tight curls. Now Sophia was au-
burn, Michaela streaky blonde, and Miranda completely
blonde. Only Esther and Sean were still dark. With the exception of Michaela, they were all recognizably Jewish.
There was something about Michaela, perhaps her height,
that posed a question regarding her ethnic origins. She was
also the least observant and had "married out." Her children
were raised as Catholics, the faith of their father.

Sophia looked from one to the other of her siblings with
a loving gaze; at the same time, she asked herself how much
of what she felt for them was based on their shared history.
Could she really say she knew them these days? They had
such different lives and barely had any interests in common. Look at Michaela, she thought. Had she always been
so blunt? Her attitude toward their father verged on being
stupid, although she clearly was not that.

Michaela briefly opened her eyes and looked at her older
sister. She had not been asleep. She was thinking how different her life was in comparison to her siblings, and yet there
were these ties—something that pulled her back to them and
gave her strength as she became older. In some ways, none
of them had changed. Sophia was still the best looking she
thought, though the red hair was a mistake. She still knew
how to dress and how to get people to do her bidding. Even
though she lived thousands of miles away, she was the one
who had made sure they were all aware of the funeral arrangements that had been organized by their Aunt Alicia.

Michaela thought she should have been the one to plan
it. She lived closest to their mother and saw her two or three
times a week. She was with her mother when she had the
heart attack, She had called the ambulance and was with her
when she died. Thereafter, Michaela admitted, she had panicked and called Sophia to come home and take over. She
could have called Miranda but she would have just upset everyone and would forget to do things. Sean could arrange
Mr. X's funeral when the time came, if he wanted to, and
leave her out of it please! Esther was too tied up with her

pathetic husband and her mummy's boys, which brought her to question why none of the spouses had attended.

Sophia's Jake could not leave his job, and Miranda's David was in the hospital having his varicose veins removed. She excused her own Harry on the grounds that he was not Jewish and had never participated in her family's side of things, but what about Sean's wife and Esther's Adrian? Sean had said something about Deborah coming separately and meeting them there with her mother and other wailing relatives. Adrian, of course, could not leave the boys while Mummy was absent.

The one time Michaela had fallen out with her mother was about Miriam marrying another actor as if Eli Rosen hadn't been one too many. It had led to a fairly lengthy period of estrangement in which Michaela refused to speak to either of her parents. Although she was very unhappy about it, she would never have admitted it. One of the many characteristics Michaela shared with her mother, whom she adored, was the ability to gloss over the unpleasant things in her life and to pretend they never happened—to the point that she believed it. After Michael Katz left, Miriam and Michaela were once again best friends, united in their scorn for Eli Rosen, his concert parties, and annual pantomimes. They always referred to him as Mr. X. It was a pity that Harry had never got along with her mother, although the same could be said of all the spouses.

She looked at the other occupants of the car on this interminable journey and experienced a sense of regret that she did not know them better. She rather admired Sophia who had managed never to fall out with any of them. She could have resented her because she was smart and good-looking, had interesting children, and had married twice to achieving husbands. But she felt nothing but love and respect.

Miranda was a different kettle of fish, quarrelsome and opinionated and, of course, filthy rich. She could have afforded to help their mother more, but David kept a tight purse and nothing could be spent without his permission.

Sean was a dear person. He had suffered a lot when Miriam had left Eli—and Sean with him. But he seemed to bear no resentment and loved his mother nonetheless. Michaela knew she had teased him too much about being overemotional. It was her defence against smothering him with her own love—a love she feared he might not get at home.

As for Esther, the baby, well, she hardly knew her. Esther was in to New Age everything. This included alternative medicine and Kabbalah, as well as psychiatry, astrology, and different forms of religion—all of which Michaela dismissed as rubbish. She did concede, however, that Esther was a good mother and ensured that her two sons were culturally and academically well educated. A bit overprotective, bless her, but very caring. It made Michaela wonder what had gone wrong with her own two girls, but she was not about to dwell on it. She noticed that Esther was staring at her, and the disturbing thought came to her that perhaps New Age believers could read the minds of others.

Actually, Esther was thinking how much she loved all her sisters—particularly Sophia, who was her role model. Although all the sisters had overtaken the eldest in height and girth, Sophia was always thought of as "the big sister." As long as Esther could remember, she had never received a cross word from her loving big sister. Although she very much approved of Sophia's second husband Jake, an Israeli investment analyst, she was more upset than she had ever said when they had moved to San Francisco. Even with some fifteen years between Esther and Sophia, they were the closest of the sisters in looks and interests. She really missed their get-togethers and the strength and comfort these gave her. She readily acknowledged that hers had been the most privileged of infancies. As the youngest, she was loved and treasured by everyone including both parents. She had always regarded herself as the weakling of the tribe, the one who needed guidance and protection.

However, she was strong enough to be the rock on which her own family had been built. Despite the ridicule of some of her siblings, she had pursued an interest in alternative faiths and lifestyles. She was thinking about this as she looked at Michaela who regularly poured scorn on her beliefs. One might say that scorn was Michaela's forte, yet Esther loved her as she did all her sisters. Michaela was a Sagittarius so probably couldn't help it.

Esther, whose depth and perceptions were greater than any of her siblings had ever given her credit for, was always quick to find excuses for the behaviour of others. She possessed the strongest familial sense and had battled on their behalf with Adrian more times than she would ever tell. Most of their arguments had arisen from her husband's criticism of the woman they were now about to dispach to the afterlife. It hurt her to hear him denounce the way Miriam had left Sean and their father and had taken her, Esther, away from them without a word of explanation or preparation. In truth, she knew he was right, but it didn't help her come to terms with it to hear him say it. And so she defended Miriam's actions.

A gentle soul, Esther always preferred calm and stability to discord and confrontation. So the arguments with Adrian were few and far between and never when the boys were around. She was protective of her children and home schooled the younger son, after he had suffered some bullying at the local school

In an untypical period of silence, Esther looked from one of her siblings to the other as they made their way to Chichester. She wondered whether any one of them was affected as much as she was by the sudden rupture of their family. She doubted it. Yes, Sean must have suffered when his mother left, but he had always been closer to their father, and his career had taken him away from home. Sophia and Michaela had already left home and Miranda was in boarding school.

For Esther, it had meant the loss of her father and brother overnight when she was only six years old. She never lived with them again. Her goal was to make sure this didn't happen in her family. Her family was the driving force of her life.

And what drove her brother? She could see that he was unhappy. It was etched in his face. What she didn't know was whether it was unhappiness at their mother's unexpected death or whether it was his general state. As she made up her mind that she should make more of an effort to see him and his family, he caught her eye and smiled.

Sean had been thinking about Esther and how well she had survived what had happened to them. By all accounts, she was a great mother and an exceptional social worker despite a late start in her career. She had been a conspicuously bright child, so it was a pity she had never made it to university. He resolved to ask her about it. Perhaps she could still attend now that the boys were growing up.

Sean had never had aspirations to go to university. He knew his limitations. He had tried to explain them often enough to his teachers, but it did not help that he was Sophia Rosen's brother. He had been expected to follow in her brilliant footsteps, but the only subject in which he could hold his own was maths He had been able to turn that to good effect in a moderately successful career in accounting. It suited him and, as it turned out, someone had recommended him to Deborah's parents. A combination of his good looks, steady employment, and impeccable, if somewhat unconventional Jewish credentials, had made him a marriageable prospect.

He and Deborah had been married now for more than twenty years. Like Esther and Adrian, he and Deborah had two boys now at university. Deborah had returned to teaching special education children locally so that she would have the same holiday breaks as her boys. If Sean had been asked to rate his happiness, he would immediately cite nine out of ten. If he had time to think about it more deeply, he would have lowered it a bit. Only Deborah knew that Sean had been through intensive therapy to shed his conviction that if he had been less of an academic disappointment, his mother would never have left home when he was just eleven.

He had been urged to discuss it with Miriam but had never dared to; he feared she would confirm his worst fears. Even the therapy failed to convince him that he was not to blame for what had happened. He was the only son and that surely vested in him a special responsibility for his mother's happiness. Instead, she had left him without saying goodbye or explaining why she was leaving. That alone assured him that he must have done something wrong. She was a good, kind woman who loved her children—what other explanation could there be? It never occurred to him to shift the blame to his mother let alone condemn her, even though he had heard nothing from her until he was thirteen. Two years had passed; two years that he preferred not to think about. Two years when he and his father had divided up the household chores between them and lived on snacks until his own attempts at cooking improved. But Miriam did not forget his bar mitzvah. She had sent him a generous amount of money and, as was her style, a note that avoided all the issues. He would rather have had her come to the service and the little party Eli had arranged than receive money. But he was happy to have heard from her, and he forgave her absence by telling everyone that she would have come if she didn't have a new husband.

Now, that husband was gone and so was Miriam. He would never be able to ask her why she had left. Looking around at his sisters, he thought that one day he might talk to Miranda about it. They were the closest in age and had kept in touch. As if she had read his thoughts, Miranda leaned over and touched him on the knee. She smiled at him and asked, "Are you okay?" He nodded yes.

"I'd like to talk to you when this is all over," he said.

Miranda would not have called herself a deep thinker, but she was concerned about her brother. She was a practical woman who just got on with her life, and like Michaela, she tended to dismiss psychological explanations. Nevertheless, on this day, when they had all gathered together to say their final farewells to their mother, she too reflected on her childhood. And as she had done during infrequent, quiet moments, she wondered how Sean had fared emotionally. On the surface he seemed fine, but she couldn't believe he was unscathed.

There had been a time, after she had left school and realized she had no home to return to, when she had taken a live-in job at a stable so that she could be near her mother and little sister while indulging her passion for horses. She had wanted to ask Miriam how she could have left Sean and why she was not in touch with him, but she feared a hostile reaction and things were difficult enough as they were. After that, she had reservations about probing into Sean's feelings. So, somehow, they had never faced what was undoubtedly a trauma for all of them. Sophia and Michaela, the two eldest, may have been spared somewhat as they had already left home—Sophia to university, Michaela to marriage at age eighteen.

The breakup of her home certainly affected Miranda despite trying to believe otherwise. She could live anywhere with anyone and that, for a few years, is what she did. After working with horses, she took a series of *au pair* jobs, sometimes doubling as secretary and personal assistant. She preferred not to think about those years when at least one of the positions she held had become too personal and she had been shown the door by an angry wife. This was followed by an extraordinary sequence of boyfriends of various nationalities and hues, including one who eventually became a millionaire pop star. She used to say that her theme song was "another suitcase in another hall." She was, by far, the most sexually experienced of the Rosen girls. This was one of the reasons why her siblings were astonished when she settled down with steady, quiet, well-employed David Dickenson. It turned out to be a most successful marriage.

Miranda looked from one to the other of her siblings. They were all parents, and Miranda couldn't help but wonder whether she and David would have been as happy with one another if they had children. After several miscarriages, they accepted that they would be a family without children. They did not want to adopt, and they had numerous nieces and nephews. They comforted themselves with a series of beloved animals and decided to go into business together. They began by running a pub and, over the years, moved on to larger and more successful restaurants. Now they were media restaurateurs and controlled a chain of well-reviewed places to eat and, in two cases, to sleep.

There was not much in her life she regretted, Miranda thought to herself as she regarded her siblings. If she was strictly honest, there were times when she had wished she could take back certain words that had escaped from her lips. Her sharp tongue had landed her in trouble more than once—especially with her sister, Michaela, her closest competitor in the acerbic stakes. There had been a time when they had not spoken to one another for years, but today she could barely remember what it had been about.

She was fortunate in many ways to have married David, only one of which was his ability to laugh at her sarcasm. In all their years together, she could recall only one serious quarrel when he had been hurt by something she had said. She had been foolish enough to be unkind about his sexual prowess with its implied comparison with lovers in her past. But that was a long time ago and she had learned from it. She valued David's goodness too much to risk a repetition and so they had gone from strength to strength both in their relationship and in the competitive world of catering.

Miranda's thoughts turned to the occupant in the car in front of them. She had endeavoured to remain friends with both her parents after they split up, but she had seen much more of Miriam. She had fallen out with her mother many times, but they had always made up—as she had with Michaela. Those two were so alike, she sighed, obstinate, self-deluding, and at the worst, self-satisfied. Had she been a bit jealous of their closeness? Perhaps. And yet she reckoned she had been more tolerant of their mother's capriciousness than any of the others. In a way, she even admired it. You had to respect a woman who retained a free spirit after bearing five children, going through two divorces. and living more often than not near the bread line. This was why she had not complained about Miriam's choice of funeral ceremony and location, a place they seemed to be approaching as the hearse in front of them reverted to its slower rate of progress.

The siblings simultaneously became aware that the journey to Chichester was nearing its end. The grey drizzle that had accompanied their departure had cleared leaving a watery sky with a few halfhearted shafts of sun. As the hearse turned into the tree-lined drive of their destination, each of the five siblings, without saying a word to one another, experienced similar emotions. They all were nervous about the imminent and unfamiliar ceremony. They were determined to keep their feelings under control, if only for the sake of the others. And each one, even Michaela, was thinking that their father should be present.

Chapter Two

The funeral cars made their sedate way round a circular drive lined with rose bushes before stopping in front of the crematorium chapel.

"Who the hell are all these people?" Michaela whispered to Sophia as she gestured toward the crowd assembled in small groups in front of the building.

"They look like *artistes*, if you ask me," Sophia replied with a sarcastic reference to the term used by their father for his fellow performers.

"Christ help us," her sister said as Esther gave her a nudge, indicating that she had yet again used unsuitable vocabulary.

"Look, there's Auntie Alicia," Michaela pointed out, "over there at the back."

"At least we know one person here."

"Deborah should be somewhere, with her mum and some of her folk," Sean added as the siblings emerged from the funeral car and waited uncertainly for someone in charge to tell them what they were supposed to do next.

"Deborah's with Alicia and they're coming over here," Miranda said. "And, oh Jesus, ex-Uncle Greg is with her. What's he doing here?"

"Mum always used to say that he proposed to her before he settled for Alicia, so maybe he's heartbroken," Michaela observed.

"I hope he's not going to be embarrassing," Esther said looking up from scanning her mobile phone for messages.

"For heaven's sake, Esther. This whole thing is going to be embarrassing, so just be prepared," said Michaela.

Sophia drew a deep breath and turned to her sisters and brother. "Look, Michaela's probably right but we have to be on our best behaviour. Remember what Dad used to say— sorry Michaela—chin up, shoulders back, you're beautiful, you're confident, and you are the star."

As she completed her sentence, Sophia felt someone grab her around the waist from behind. She turned to face her mother's sister Alicia who was surrounded by a few familiar and many more unfamiliar faces.

"Sophia, darling," Alicia said reaching up to kiss her. Sophia was not that tall but Alicia was shorter by at least three inches. Alicia was Miriam's older sister by four years but had lived a quieter and more conventional life. There was a little something of Miriam about her—but not enough of a reminder to upset the siblings.

"Look at all of you," Alicia said. "How many years is it since I've seen you all together? I must say you haven't changed much. It is such a pity we have to wait for an occasion like this to be together."

She then grabbed her former husband by the arm and pulled him forward.

"You remember your Uncle Greg, don't you?"

She proceeded to kiss each one of them on both cheeks while Uncle Greg hung back, not so much being embarrassing as being embarrassed.

Meanwhile, Deborah had moved to Sean's side followed by a few Deborah look-a-likes who turned out to be her mother and two sisters. After the introductory kissing and handshaking, no one seemed to know what to say. The usual greetings seemed to be out of order; no one wanted to be too cheerful or hearty. There was an understandable reluctance to tell Miriam anecdotes. The murmured phrase that went around the waiting crowd was "died tragically young."

Miriam was at least seventy-nine years old when the final, fatal heart attack struck. Her death could hardly have been called "tragic" unless heavy smoking counted as the fatal flaw of which tragedy is made. She had suffered several minor warning attacks, and after each she swore to her doctor and her children that no cigarette would ever be found between her lips again. But she cheated often and like her mother, sister, and brothers before her, she had paid the price. Two difficult marriages, many pregnancies, five live births, and never enough money also could be assumed to have taken their toll.

"I've asked Sean to say a few words. Is that alright with you?"

Alicia looked anxiously at her eldest niece. "I thought you wouldn't mind as you spoke at Rosa's funeral."

Sophia couldn't help an irreverently comic thought passing through her mind at Alicia's words. The idea that the siblings were to take turns in speaking at the older generations' funerals was a touch bizarre, but she managed to stop herself from asking her aunt to nominate the guest speaker at her own funeral. Instead she replied, "It's fine Auntie, as long as Sean agrees and feels he's up to it. He's been a bit tearful all morning. Anyway, who are all these people and what can we expect to happen?"

Sophia thought she detected a slight uneasiness in Alicia's response to her question. "Which people? Oh those," as Sophia gestured towards a group standing apart from the family. "They are your mother's Chichester friends, people from the theatre here."

"I see," Sophia said. "We were all wondering why she wanted to be cremated here. We didn't know about her Chichester friends."

Alicia looked alarmed and blurted, "So you don't know about Anton?"

"Who's Anton?"

Alicia moved a bit closer to Sophia and muttered, "He's the tall one wearing a grey scarf in the middle of the Chichester group."

"Don't tell me he's an actor," Sophia sighed.

"Of course he is. Anton Dolinsky. Haven't you heard of him?"

"Vaguely," Sophia replied. "But never in connection with my mother."

"I think we'd better have this conversation later on darling," Alicia said. "Okay?"

She turned and moved toward the Chichester group.

"What was all that about?" Michaela asked Sophia as soon as Alicia was out of earshot.

"Have you ever heard of Anton Dolinsky?" Sophia asked her sister.

"No. Should I have?"

"Apparently we all should have. He was, it seems, a close friend of Mum's. He's the tall one with wild hair, wearing a grey scarf. Alicia's talking to him now."

"Nice looking for an old man," was Michaela's curt response.

"We'll talk about it after this show is over. I'll try to warn the others before we have to meet him," Sophia remarked. "Oh, oh, too late," she added as she saw Alicia moving the Chichester people in their direction.

Miranda and Esther were talking to Deborah and her family when, by some inaudible signal, they moved toward their older sisters as Alicia and the Chichester group homed in on them. Alicia, behaving like a nervous hostess, announced to one and all. "I would like you to meet Miriam's children who have assembled from all over the globe to be here."

"The globe is stretching it a bit," said Michaela holding out her hand at once to Anton Dolinsky. "My name's Michaela, I'm second in the line of succession. This is my sister Sophia, who is, in fact, the only one who has really travelled. She's from San Francisco. The rest of us are more or less locals."

"You're like your mother," Anton replied with real tears in his eyes. "I'm delighted to meet you all at last." Indicating the group around him, he added, "We were all devastated to hear of her death."

"She was such a character," put in a smaller man in actorly dress of corduroy pants, denim jacket, open neck shirt, and a designer beard. "An absolute character but a darling."

"She'll be missed," added a woman who was introduced by Anton as the theatre's voice coach.

Murmurs of agreement and more handshaking followed as the bewildered siblings tried to understand what all these people had to do with their mother.

"How did you know my mother?" Miranda asked in a too bright tone. The slight pause accompanied by glances in Anton's direction was brought to an end by movement toward the chapel building that heralded the start of the proceedings.

As they made their way to the entrance, Anton said to Sophia, "So you are the eldest. Your mother was so proud of you."

"Really, was she?" Sophia answered. "She never told me."

"Ah, well," he said enigmatically. "The things we don't tell." And then he added,

"I'll be glad when this is over, won't you?"

"Actually yes," she replied. "It's a bit of an ordeal. I'm not used to cremations—

I mean," she corrected herself, "funerals. They are always difficult, but to think of one's own mother being . . . you know." She broke off feeing rather foolish and inadequate.

If, indeed, this good-looking man had been her mother's lover, he must be in a state of distress and she doubted she had made him feel any better.

"I hope you will come to the reception," he said as they made their way to the front door of the little chapel. "We've planned something special."

"I guess so," she replied.

Neither she nor her sisters and brother had known anything about a reception if "reception" was the correct word. Clearly, Alicia had arranged something about which she had, no doubt, intended to inform them when they all assembled. A touch high-handed, she thought, and possibly linked to the puzzling location and the presence of a cast of actors.

"Reception?" Sophia whispered to Alicia as she took her place alongside her with her siblings already seated on Alicia's other side. Deborah and her family sat in the row behind them. Sean looked on the verge of collapse, but the attention of all the others was focused on the front rows on the other side of the aisle.

"Who are they?" Miranda hissed, indicating the Chichester group. "And why are they in the front row?"

Michaela, who sat between Miranda and Sophia, nudged Sophia in the ribs to answer. Sophia whispered back to her sisters, "Tell you afterwards. Seems to be a long story."

All further conversation was brought to a halt by the appearance of a seriously suited man who gestured for silence. It didn't stop Michaela from saying in a not too inaudible voice, "I think he must be the presenter."

The wooden coffin draped in white silk cloth with gold tassels was centre stage. The man in the suit stood to its right. The smell of lilies was overpowering thought Sophia as Esther, who suffered from asthma, started sneezing.

"The proceedings today," began the presenter who was a stranger to the siblings, "will be somewhat unconventional at the request of the deceased. Miriam Stern Rosen seems to have been a remarkable lady, as many present today will testify.

"Though she departed from us too early, she had given much thought to the manner of her departure. She chose to be cremated though that is not the norm in Jewish circles. She chose to be cremated in the vicinity of one of her beloved theatres anticipating that her final exit from this world would be attended not only by her beloved children and their families but also by the acting fraternity that was so much a part of her life.

"By her wish, there will be no eulogies save a brief tribute from her only son. There will be no prayers or sermons of a religious nature, but there will be music. Miriam, as you all know, possessed a fine soprano voice, which in her younger years delighted audiences at the Savoy Theatre. She requested that her departure be accompanied by the overture to Verdi's opera, *La Traviata*. Thus, there will be no further words from me. I will now ask Sean to say a few words before his mother goes to her eternal rest accompanied by Verdi's immortal music."

The sisters looked from one to the other in bewilderment as Sean stepped up to stand next to the coffin. He made a supreme effort to control his emotions as he told the assembled audience that he spoke on behalf of his sisters to bid farewell to a mother who was indeed unconventional but was loved nonetheless for that. He explained that she had made many sacrifices in order to raise a large family but had clung to her individuality throughout. There had been hard, even deprived times but she never lost her spirit. If he had to define her in one word he would choose "resourceful." He remembered that as a child, his class had been asked to write a card in school for Mother's Day. The best had been read aloud during an end-of-year concert. When his was read, his mother had cried. It said, "I love my mother because she makes me laugh." After a brief pause, Sean added, "But today, I am not laughing. I will miss her."

As he sat down, the strains of Verdi's overture began and the coffin started to move backward into a cavity that appeared at the back of the chapel. Copious sobs and sniffles came from the front rows across the aisle. Alicia and Sean were crying. But the four sisters were dry-eyed, too stunned to break down and too confused for emotion.

When the coffin had completely disappeared, the presenter said in hushed tones,

"That is the end of this brief ceremony. The ashes will be given to her sister, Alicia, in order for her to carry out the remainder of Miriam's wishes. Drive home safely."

After a brief pause, Michaela said to Sophia, "Did you know anything about all these wishes?"

"No, did you?"

"Of course not. But someone did. It must be Alicia. She should have told us."

"Maybe there was no time. Mum wasn't expected to die you know."

"What was all that about?" Miranda asked as they filed out of the chapel. "What a weird funeral."

"What do we do now?" asked Esther. "I'm all goose bumps."

"Sean darling," Sophia said giving her brother a hug as he caught up with them. "You were wonderful. I know it wasn't easy for you."

"You were great," Deborah echoed, linking arms with her husband. "I thought you'd break down but you were fine."

"I prepared it, of course," Sean modestly admitted. "But I wasn't at all ready for everything else—the music, the Houdini bit with the coffin. Dad would have approved of that. He met Houdini, you know."

"Oh yeah, yeah, yeah," Michaela mocked. "Like he knew Laurel and Hardy and Sammy Davis Junior. Anyway, why are we talking about him? He was not the corpse at this funeral."

"Steady on, Michaela," Sophia cautioned. "Sean's right. What went on in there would definitely have appealed to Dad—very theatrical and actually very moving if we'd been prepared for it. Anyway, there's something I need to tell you all before we catch up with Alicia. It's alright Debs. You can stay," she said, as Deborah seemed inclined to move back to her mother and family, perhaps feeling she would be out of place.

Now in a small group outside the chapel, the family clustered around Sophia.

"It seems," Sophia started, "that Mum had a relationship with Anton Dolinsky, the tall actor with the scarf and a beard who sat with the theatre crowd in the front row opposite us. Alicia told me just before we went in, and I spoke to him briefly. I don't know how long it had been going on, but he is clearly very upset and it no doubt explains why Mum wanted to be cremated here. Anyway, I thought I had better put you in the picture before we go to the reception."

"What reception?" Esther asked.

"I think Alicia is about to tell us," Michaela said as they saw their aunt approaching them.

"Ask her to tell us the rest," Miranda suggested.

"What's the point?" Sean grumbled. "Mum's dead and it is all history. I don't really want to know. I suppose we have to go to whatever it is?"

"Yes, you do," Alicia said as she joined them, evidently having overheard Sean's last words. "Of course you do. The company has laid on a nice spread at the theatre. You have to be there."

"Tell us about Mum and this Anton," Miranda demanded. "We know nothing about it. None of us ever heard her mention him, and I can't remember her saying she was visiting Chichester."

"I can't really go into details now, love. But I will, I promise. I think your mum was perfectly well aware that none of you wanted her to get involved with yet another actor. And she was entitled to her little secrets, don't you think? Don't you all have them? He's very nice, and I believe he loved her. That should be enough shouldn't it? Now come along all of you. He's longing to get to know you all and so are the others."

"So you knew all about it, Alicia. It's one helluva a big secret if you ask me," Miranda said. "When exactly did you know?"

"Only recently. I think your mother had a premonition about dying. She shared more in the past two years. Rosa also knew.

I'm surprised she didn't tell you Sophia. You two were always so close."

Alicia ushered them to their car. "You'd better follow me," she called out as she moved toward her own car.

"Did she tell you?" Miranda asked Sophia as they settled back in the car.

"No she didn't," Sophia replied. "I only just learned about Mum and this Anton from Alicia. Aunt Rosa was very protective of me and our mother. Anyway, it's not the kind of thing she would have told me on the phone or in a letter. Maybe if I'd seen her every week like I used to, she would have said something, but after I went abroad, it wasn't the same. How could it be? The last time I saw her was in a wooden box like Mum's."

With that said, Sophia shed her tears. It's wrong, she thought. I'm crying for my dead aunt and not for my dead mother. It's all wrong.

The others noticed. They all knew why Sophia cried for Rosa. They understood, but they said nothing.

Finally Esther said, "How long do you think we have to stay?"

"Anxious to get back home already?" Michaela teased her.

"Well yes, frankly. I don't fancy being at a party just after our mother's been reduced to ashes, especially if there's going to be a lot of nudge, nudge, wink, wink."

"I don't think there'll be any of that," Sean said. "These theatrical people are used to affairs and different behaviours aren't they? They're probably just curious to look over Miriam's offspring."

"That's what I mean, really," Esther replied. "It's all a bit too weird for me."

"Speaking of ashes," Miranda suddenly joined in. "What did that guy in the suit mean when he said Mum's ashes would be given to Alicia to carry out her final wishes or whatever?"

"She probably wanted them preserved to be mingled with Anton's when the time comes and scattered backstage in the Chichester Theatre or affixed in an urn to a pedestal in the Theatre Museum in Covent Garden," observed Michaela.

"Don't be horrible, Michaela," Sophia admonished. "We'll ask Alicia."

The remainder of the journey passed in silence as each of the siblings internalized what they had just witnessed and what they had just learned. From time to time, they exchanged glances, smiled at one another with love and the unspoken acknowledgement of the commonality of their thoughts. The recognition of a shared memory bound them one to the other, however far apart they lived, however their tastes and practices differed. They left the car and entered the Chichester Theatre restaurant as one body, the offspring of Miriam and Eli Rosen. But were family memories really shared?

Are they ever?

Part Two: Sophia's Version

Chapter Three

It was my Aunt Alicia who told me how Rosa had died. Her narrative continues to haunt me, which is a pity because all my other memories of Rosa are loving and happy.

Alicia told me, "Rosa had been screaming, 'give me a cigarette. For God's sake someone give me a cigarette!' And, if I'd had one, I would have ignored the signs everywhere and given it to her. What harm could it have done her at that stage? Or anyone else there for that matter? They were all dying. But this big fat nurse, who stank of garlic and disinfectant, came over to the bed and said to me, 'Can't you keep your sister quiet?' And then she leaned over Rosa, who, of course, couldn't see her but she could smell her alright and scolded her, 'If someone had told you no cigarettes a year ago, you silly woman, you wouldn't have had both your legs chopped off. Now be quiet. Yelling won't do you any good.'"

"Then Rosa reached out and took my hand," Alicia continued, "and I saw tears rolling down her face. She uttered only six more words before she died. She said, 'Tell my girl I love her.' Two hours later she was gone."

Her "girl" was me. Until the day I join her, if that is what happens, I will regret that I was not at her bedside to hear her say those words. I was not at the hospital because I was in India. My husband had to go on a business visit, and I wanted to go with him. But I knew Rosa was ill. So I consulted her surgeon.

"Of course, you must go," he said. "I can't tell you how much time your aunt has left. Maybe days, maybe weeks. You can't live your life according to the clock that is ticking away for her. All I can tell you is that she will never leave the hospital."

His words cut into me, although I knew they made sense. Rosa was blind. Her husband was blind. She would have no legs and their flat was much too small for her to manipulate a wheelchair in even if that was possible. She was only 68 and would not live much longer.

I had been home from New Delhi just two hours when my uncle's call came. And home was not London where Rosa's body lay, but San Francisco. And, like almost everyone else on the plane coming back, I had raging dysentery.

"I have to go to London," I told my husband.

"I understand," he said. "I'll call the travel agent."

He helped me take the things I needed out of one case and put them in another, That evening I boarded another plane to make the most difficult journey of my life.

As a young child, I believe I really thought Rosa was my mother. You hear a lot of talk these days about the importance of bonding with your baby from its earliest days. Well, I bonded with Rosa without anyone realizing it.

My mother was just seventeen years old when I was born—perfectly in wedlock. My parents had married when my mother was just legally old enough with her father's consent. Rosa had celebrated her nineteenth birthday only three days before my arrival. She was my mother's half sister. Her father died before Rosa was born and his best friend, who was a lodger in my grandmother's house, took pity on her with her four children and Rosa on the way, and married her. My mother was born when Rosa was eighteen months old.

At this distance in time, it is difficult for me to describe Rosa as she must have been when I first became aware of her as the most important person in my life. I only recall impressions of a tall, dark, boney presence smelling of cigarettes leaning over me speaking in a quiet gentle voice full of love. Her presence meant security, warmth, and comfort. She always seemed to be there.

She was, in fact, tall, dark, and boney. My mother was notoriously short and, as she grew older, increasingly plump. Rosa was the tallest of the women in my family and as thin as a beanpole except, as I remember on the one occasion when I saw her in shorts, for her rather sturdy legs. The bones of her hands and shoulders stood out and I used to trace the hollows in her collarbone with my small fingers.

Her almost black hair, which she coloured black long after she should have, came to a point in the middle of her forehead. She explained to me this was called a "widow's peak." And of course, I had to ask if that meant she would be a widow. She hoped not and, indeed, she never was. Her white skin was very soft—especially around her high cheekbones. But her eyes described her character the best. Before the cataracts and the blindness, they were the kindest, softest, sparkling green eyes that looked at me with devotion. Later, the colour faded but the expression around them never did.

I was born in the reign of Edward VIII. Not many people can say that as he reigned less than a year. My mother gave me life, but I was literally Rosa's baby from the moment I was born into her arms in my grandmother's house. I was born on a Thursday. Rosa had also been born on a Thursday. She attached great significance to the fact that we were both Thursday's children. The night I was born, my father was appearing at the Hippodrome New Brighton.

After I was born, my mother was anxious to get back on stage as a young chorister with the D'Oyly Carte Opera Company. So it suited everyone that I should be placed in the care of Rosa and my grandmother. And that's how it was until the day that forms my first memory. I remember screaming as my arms were pulled from around Rosa's neck and I was sent with my mother and my new baby sister to a northern destination because the Germans were about to invade Britain—or so everyone believed.

My mother had decided I was to be called Scarlett. Rosa put up a fight about this and won. "You cannot call a child with the surname Rosen, Scarlett," she said. And of course, she was right

It wasn't only that I appeared to have two mothers—three if you count my grandmother—that gave me a feeling of being different even at an early age. It was also the strong sense of existing in a large bubble of love surrounded by a sea of disapproval. It was clear to me that Grandmother Stern—by name and by nature as she used to quip—and Rosa, to a lesser extent, disapproved of my father and all he represented. These two strong women felt it their clear duty to protect me from his influence even if Miriam, my mother, was a lost cause. My father's major fault was that his mother was not Jewish. It would have been something very different if my grandfather on my father's side, who was Jewish, had not been so keen to hide his heritage. He had journeyed as a young man from Poland to Cork in the south of Ireland where, in the belief that it was the promised New York, he disembarked to start a new life. Somewhere in the years it took him to move from Cork to Dublin, Moshe Rosinsky became Mathew Rosen. Once in Dublin's fair city, he met and married an Irish Catholic girl with a mass of black curly hair and, according to the Stern family legend, no shoes on her feet!

Eli Rosen, the first child of this union and later to be my father, joined Dublin's Abbey Theatre as a stage carpenter. He was granted occasional parts as a walk-on, usually in the role of a Jew for which his Semitic looks made him an obvious choice. He left Dublin, like generations of his countrymen before and after him, with big ambitions, no money, and an almost pathological hatred of the religion in which his mother had raised him.

He migrated to London in search of work in the theatre and met Miriam Stern, my mother, auditioning for a singing part in the same production. According to my mother, they fell instantly in love, although Rosa's version was more along the lines of a stage struck and innocent young girl who was deluded into thinking that a handsome Irish-Jewish actor was bound to become a star. The truth most likely lay somewhere between the two versions, but they did marry.

By everyone's account, and certainly according to the evidence, the marriage turned out to be a mistake. The outbreak of the war put an end to Eli's career and whatever had been in the relationship for Miriam ended as well. My grandmother summed it up in her oft-repeated phrase, "It was no more nor less than could have been expected. Marrying a *goyische* actor at age sixteen and having all those children with outlandish names not to mention the horror of an Irish family with, no doubt, Romany origins, it was bound to end in disaster." So ran the conversation at Stern family gatherings over the years, usually in lowered voices on account of my presence.

But oddly enough, the disaster took a good many years to arrive. I was only three when Rosa told me after my bedtime story, "My darling, Mummy, baby Michaela and you are going to have to go on a train to somewhere safe. But only for the duration." The words that stayed with me from listening to adult conversations were *blitzkrieg* and *duration* neither of which I understood. But even at that tender age, I realized that neither these words nor the other recurrent words, *Hilter* and *the North,* were good news. Rosa, my grandmother, and my mother all cried a great deal, so I figured the duration was going to last a long time and it somehow penetrated my child's brain that it would not be a good idea to join in the crying.

But when it came time for the point of departure, and it became clear to me that Rosa was not to accompany us, my resolve broke down and the rafters of Euston Station rang to my screams. No provisions had been made for Rosa and my grandmother to avoid Hitler's bombs. All this I truly remember though I am told it is most unlikely in a child so young. I remember the carriage. I remember that my father was not there. I remember Michaela was tightly wrapped, as babies were in those days, in a white knitted shawl. I do not remember the journey, but I have a clear recollection of arriving. We stopped after what seemed like a very long time at a small railway station with just two tracks—one coming and one going.

"Where are we?" several women asked, leaning out of the windows and looking for signs.

A man in uniform said something that made the mothers laugh—very possibly for the first time since they had left London and their loved ones. I later learned that the train's destination was a place in northeast Lancashire called Ramsbottom. No wonder it raised a laugh.

It was intensely cold. The man in uniform was joined by a group of people carrying clipboards. Voices were shouting directions and telling us to take our belongings and board the buses that were outside the station. Snow was everywhere. It came over my shoes and made my already cold feet colder and wet. I was also very hungry, but one look at my mother's face told me not to complain. She and the other women around us were not shouting or complaining but they were subdued and looked frightened as well they might. They had not been told where we were going, what the living conditions would be, or how long we would be there.

I do believe that the only reason Grandmother Stern and Rosa had submitted to the government's plan for getting young women and children out of the capital before the expected *blitzkrieg* began, was that my Aunt Alicia was already "somewhere in the north" with her son Jacob. The plan was for Miriam, Michaela, and me to join her. My mother had an address in a village called Crawshawbooth in the Valley of Rossendale, which she handed to one of the kind volunteers who were desperately trying to calm and organize the evacuees. That was another term with which I was to become very familiar in the years that followed, since, as I had suspected, the duration turned out to be somewhat lengthier than a fortnight.

The very name Crawshawbooth sounded like a foreign place in a gruesome fairy tale or some Icelandic outpost. The plentiful snow, which I don't think I'd ever seen before, added to the impression of isolation and a frozen wilderness where few had ever set foot. Strangers kept trying to take me by the hand because my mother had a baby in one arm and her other arm was engaged in a struggle with a large suitcase. She had to let me make out for myself, and I preferred it to allowing someone I didn't know to take charge of me.

"It could be worse," the women kept saying to one another. And indeed it could. For without their knowing it, the situation of thousands of women across Europe, not to mention those left in London, Coventry, Manchester, Liverpool, and other large cities, was to become indescribably worse. As confused, cold, tired, and miserable as the evacuees were, we turned out to be the lucky ones.

Quite a number of the children and not a few of the women were crying. But I didn't cry. Could I, at three-years-old, have figured that it was pointless? My mother, far from being grateful for my reticence, commented, "That child is not natural."

Things began to look up a bit when the bus we were on stopped and someone called out, "Rosen family—this is your stop." Alicia was waiting for us with warm hugs and kisses. She gathered me up in her arms. I noticed she had the same smell as Rosa and my grandmother, a mixture of cigarettes and essence of violets, a favourite perfume of the family. Smoking appeared to be *de rigueur* in those days. Many claimed it calmed their nerves during the air raids. Maybe it did. Alicia gave it up after the war, but my mother, Rosa, and grandmother never could quit, and it cost them dearly later. I clung to my Aunt Alicia enjoying the familiar smell and being warmed up, but then she had to put me down in order to take our suitcase.

"First of all, my loves," she said. "We are going to a neighbour's house.

She's looking after Jake for me." My cousin Jake was a year younger than me, which was probably why he cried all the time. "We've been allocated a back-to-back in Stoneholme Terrace. It's not bad. A bit on the cold side, but we are lucky to have it all to ourselves.

As we negotiated our way through the snow, in the dark, I wondered what a back-to-back house was and whether Stoneholme Terrace was warmer than outside and contained food. To reach it, we had to go down what Alicia called the cat steps. I was learning new phrases by the minute. This time though, the meaning was clear. Only a cat could have descended those steps with ease especially as they were covered in ice.

"I put salt down an hour ago," Alicia said. "But they've frozen again." She went first with the suitcase, then she came back to take the baby from my mother who followed holding my hand and the flimsy rope railing with equally terrified strength. Alicia lifted the latch on a wooden gate that led into a cluttered yard. Another latched door led into a blessedly warm and welcoming kitchen where the neighbour turned out to be a hugely fat EastEnder apparently called 'Obbs.

"'Allo darlin'. I'm 'Obbs," she said to me as she gathered me to her rather smelly bosom.

"This is my sister, Miriam," Alicia said to 'Obbs, "with Sophia and baby Michaela.

"And this is Florrie Hobbs, who's been so good to us all. How's Jake, Florrie?

Has he been good?"

"Aw, he's a lovely bit of shit, that boy. Good as gold ain't you my lovely," 'Obbs replied giving Jake, who was hiding behind Alicia's legs, a pull on his ear. She went on for my mother's benefit. "This is a bloody foreign country. You won't understand a word. For instance, those things you're standing on," she said while pointing to the stone floor, "are called flags if you don't mind! Things that go on poles, not on the bloody floor." My mother's frowning and trying surreptitiously to cover my ears didn't shield me a bit. I was to hear plenty of it. And I certainly liked 'Obbs despite her sweaty smell and the cups of strong, very sweet tea she insisted we all drink, before we went anywhere, when we arrived, when we returned, and on receipt of any kind of news good or bad. Considering that tea, milk, and sugar were rationed at the time, 'Obbs had a mysteriously plentiful supply of all three. We were soon to learn that the redoubtable 'Obbs was the head cook and bottle washer of the Crawshawbooth evacuees and definitely a good person to know.

I don't think I had ever drunk tea before but there was no resisting 'Obbs commands. I drank it on that first cold night in our new home and was glad for it.

It was virtually the only warm thing I remember about that time. Alicia collected Jake and we all thanked 'Obbs and her grandson George, who had appeared from the recesses of the back-to-back when he smelled the tea, and moved off to Alicia's house two doors away.

It appeared that Stoneholme Terrace had been requisitioned *en bloc* to accommodate the evacuees. Eventually, a little Cockney community formed and the residents lived through each other's traumas, swapping bread units for clothing coupons, doing one another's hair, and reading each other's letters from home and from the war front. The adults were, of course, all women who very soon became the centre of local male attention with the occasional disastrous results.

The house we had been allocated was a replica of the one 'Obbs and her backward grandson George occupied. I didn't know, of course, that George was backward, or rather, I didn't know what the term meant. As far as I was concerned, George was about my age, which was more or less true except in the chronological sense. He liked to play the games I did, he understood what I was saying, which was more than could be said of the local children, and I became an expert at interpreting the noises he made. People would ask me what George had said, and I interpreted to George's delight. It made 'Obbs love me and I loved her back. She could never replace Rosa who was so different, but she made up for my mother's obsessive devotion to Michaela and Alicia's caring, but undemonstrative, nature.

I had a feeling that there was something Jewish about 'Obbs—a feeling I always meant to check with my mother or Alicia but never got around to it. In any event, as far as we knew, we were the only genuine Jews in the party, although it never became an issue. We were not observant Jews, and Miriam Rosen and her two infant daughters probably passed as being of Irish descent. Concerning Aunt Alicia Berman and her son Jacob, no assumptions were made at all. The camaraderie of wartime overcame reserve, prejudice, snobbery, and suspicion. These women were all in the same boat. Only the liaisons formed with the local men occasionally broke the spirit.

The little house we had been allocated along the row from 'Obbs was cold. Everything was cold. I remember cold stone floors, cold stone stairs, cold water to wash in, cold hands undressing me. Alicia had used her bread units to make us sandwiches with some strong tasting cold meat. I went to bed in a garment they called a siren suit, a zip-up jump suit like a modern baby-grow outfit with a hood. In London, I had worn it to bed in case we were awakened in the night and taken to the air-raid shelter. Now I wore it as protection against the cold. It was green and I loved it. I never wanted to take it off.

Things must have improved when spring came, but I don't remember that. I remember very little of my first year as an evacuee other than a terrible sense of being different and living a lonely inner life that depended more on imagination than anything that was happening around me. I was cripplingly homesick for my grandmother's house, the hot baths, and the smell of Friday cooking. Mostly I missed the warmth of Rosa's embraces and the bedtime stories she read to me. I told terrible lies to anyone who would listen, "Rosa came in a car outside Stoneholme Terrace and told me to tell you all that it is safe to come home now." I also tried, "a man told me that evacuees don't have to go to school." This was the sword of Damocles that was held over my head six months after we arrived. So I was punished and had to spend hours in the cold bedroom I shared with Jake. This gave me even more time to make up stories.

I remember my Aunt Alicia standing in front of the stone sink in the kitchen shelling peas or peeling potatoes. There always seemed to be plenty of vegetables available but not much fruit and definitely no sweets. As she worked, she wiggled her bottom, a habit she had when she was concentrating. And I remember the arrival of letters from Rosa. She usually included a postal order for me and a smaller one for Jake "because he's younger" Alicia would say with a sniff. I have no idea what happened to those postal orders.

They probably went into the household pot, but I didn't care. It was their arrival with a little note in capital letters addressed to me that mattered. "TO MY DEAREST LITTLE SOPHIA. BE A GOOD GIRL. ALL MY LOVE, ROSA."

Chapter Four

It was hard to be good. As an evacuee, I lived in a world I didn't understand and one that didn't understand me. I was waiting for the duration to come to an end and longing to be home where I belonged. So I did naughty things like hiding Jake's pathetic little wartime toys and making loud noises near Michaela's pram to wake her up. Worst of all, I stole a necklace of my mother's and gave it to a neighbour's daughter to win her friendship. This was not a particularly clever thing to do because the girl's mother brought it straight back, and I was sent to bed at four o'clock in the afternoon.

Crawshawbooth is, to this day, a small district between the towns of Rawtenstall and Burnley in northeast Lancashire where little has changed in a hundred years. It was considered safe from Hitler's bombs as being deemed not worthy of bombing. There was no industry, although it was in the middle of the cotton-processing belt. On the outskirts of the village, the fascinating remains of a mill stood testimony to more prosperous times. It was one of the several places I was forbidden to go.

As the duration stretched into years, I became old enough to walk to school on my own. The mill held a fascination for me and, disobeying orders, I spent many solitary hours there imagining what it once must have been like. I envisioned hundreds of workers wearing clogs, the women in headscarves, arriving for work and hurrying home at the sound of the factory hooter. It was a vast site with arches still standing at either end. Decipherable letters amidst the rubble indicated Danger or Exit while pretty wild flowers grew among the rampant weeds. This forbidden place made such an impression on me that it still makes frequent appearances in my dreams.

Aside from the old mill, there was little else in Crawshawbooth to linger in my memory—a pub or two, a working men's club, and a few shops. Scattered houses climbed up steep hills on either side of the main street that took children to the junior schools and carried travellers en route from Rawtenstall to Burnley. The village began abruptly at one end with the ruined mill and ended equally abruptly at the other with the police station. There must have been at least one church, but since this was not a place we set foot in, I really don't remember.

It seemed to me that if there was a social centre in Crawshawbooth, it was the butcher's shop. 'Obbs frequently held court wheedling better cuts from the butcher, Mr. Whitaker, who had a soft spot for her. The locals complained that the evacuees received more than their rations allowed because of this, but no one dared challenge either the butcher or 'Obbs the local Mother Courage. Through this odd partnership, I learned a new word. 'Obbs was hugely insulted one day because Mr. Whitaker had told her she look starved. "Bloody good luck to you," she had retorted. "I have had a good breakfast." In the Rossendale dialect, starved indicated cold in the sense of the person being freezing and not hungry as 'Obbs had understood it. It was a word used rather frequently.

I was not happy at school. I was enrolled in the local infants' school when I was four-and-one-half as the law required. It was up the cat steps and to the right. If I had felt foreign before I went to school, I was an alien among Crawshawbooth infants class A. There were other evacuees among us but not from London and definitely no other Irish Jews. On my very first day, the teacher asked me, "Are you a Catholic?"

"I don't know," I truthfully replied shivering with nerves.

My answer seemed to annoy the teacher and to amuse the kids. The other evacuees came mostly from Manchester so their manner of speech was not too different from the locals. I was apparently unintelligible.

"Why do you talk funny?" they kept asking me.

"I don't, you do," was my defiant reply. This they understood.

"Where do you come from?"

"London."

"Where's that?"

"A long way on a train."

"You tell lies."

"No I don't."

"You're a liar from London."

I would end all such encounters with the words, "I'm only here for the duration."

This established, to me and to my audience, that I was definitely not one of them and furthermore did not intend to be.

But it was obviously not a happy state of affairs. I didn't say a word to my mother or Alicia about any of this. I saved it all up to tell Rosa whenever the duration came to an end. And as time went by, there was more and more to tell.

The school was a single-storey building with a flagstone yard. Along one side of the yard, there was a row of outside toilets labelled "Boys" and "Girls." I remember one day, it must have been a year after we arrived in Crawshawbooth because it was winter again, and the ice was thick on the ground. With far greater frequency than was usual, the children in class A kept raising their hands and asking, "Please Miss, may I leave the room?" So many kids were doing this that I thought I had better do it too in case I was missing something, but maybe more significantly, because I really didn't want to be thought to be all that different.

Once outside, I saw the reason for the mass exit. The children had made a foot slide on the ice and were lining up to take a run at it. They would build up speed and then set off along the slide, one foot in front of the other, arms in the air.

I watched for a while contemplating whether or not I dare join in, but I lacked the courage to do so in front of all the others. So I just went to the toilet and returned to the classroom. After all the other children came back to their places, the teacher, looking a bit grim, suddenly commanded, "Everyone sit up straight with your arms folded."

Then she added in the cold voice of authority, "I want all those children who asked to leave the room to come up here and stand in a line facing me." About half the class, myself included, obeyed her order.

"Right," she said, "now everyone hold out their left hand."

Puzzled by this instruction, I noticed that several of the kids spat on their hands before they held them out or others pulled the sleeves of their jumpers down to cover their left hands. Then the teacher took a cane from the drawer of her desk and went along the line giving each little "rising five" hand a slap. When it came to my turn, I took my hand away before the cane struck with the result that the teacher caught her own leg with it. I waited in terror for the reaction.

She turned a furious face to me and said, "Well, little girls who can't take their punishment get a double dose. Hold out both your hands." This time I could not stop the tears.

One kid called me a cry baby as I returned to my seat. And the kids continued to taunt me when school ended,

"The evacuee is a mardy."

But I swear it was not the blow from the cane that made me cry. It was the injustice. I had done nothing except follow the crowd and go to the loo. For that, I had been punished twice.

I learned in one instant that it is not a good idea to do something because everyone else does it. The hard truth is that life is not fair. When my Aunt Alicia and Jacob met me outside the school that afternoon, I asked, "Can we wait around for a bit until all the other children have gone?"

I don't remember if she asked me why, but she concurred. I went back into the yard, screwed up my courage, and took a run at the slide. I didn't enjoy it very much, but I didn't fall over. It also made me feel better.

Most of my days in that school have passed into oblivion along with corporal punishment for even the most loutish teenage pupils.

Shortly after the caning episode, the billeting officer decided that the back-to-back in Stoneholme Terrace was too small for the two sisters and their three growing children. We moved to relatively palatial accommodation nearer to the centre of the village and my next school. The house was a large semidetached stone residence with a garden, two greenhouses, and a vine. It was called Rose Mount. None of us had ever lived in a house with a name before. The wood floors were polished, and each of us had our own bedroom.

The best thing for Jacob and me was the drawing room. It faced the hill that people going to and from the village had to pass along. It also had a piano, a fireplace, and two huge windows overlooking the hill. In no time, Jake and I had developed a very naughty game. We would knock on the windows to attract the attention of passersby and when they looked up we would poke out our tongues and then duck down below the windowsills. It says much for the tolerance of the local people that we were not caught and punished long before we were. In the end, it was a well-meaning neighbour who informed my mother that people were talking about the horrible little Jew evacuees who lived in Rose Mount, The neighbour suggested that for their own reputation, the sisters should call their children to order.

Our punishment was to be sent early to bed once again. This time, we amused ourselves by trying to dig a hole in the wall dividing the bedrooms with a hairgrip. Having longed for our own rooms, now we wanted to be able to see and speak to each other through the wall. What terrible things we did as children to the property that had been allocated to us by a kind family who had left behind their piano and velvet curtains. And I was considered to be a rule-abiding child.

The greenhouses were our favourite places to explore, especially the one with the vine that we were absolutely forbidden to enter. Our mothers made it explicitly clear that the greenhouses were dangerous. As children, we saw these as yet another new experience awaiting us. Our mothers considered the greenhouses as an unfortunate disadvantage to otherwise much-improved surroundings. But Jake and I loved the smell of the warm damp earth.

When we thought our mothers were preoccupied with the radio news or a visit from 'Obbs, we quietly sneaked out to explore the greenhouses. They were warm and enclosing. Tomatoes, with their especially pungent smell, grew well there. But it all came to an abrupt end. One day, while walking along a wall that ran alongside one of the greenhouses, I fell through a fragile glass window. I cut both legs and made a noise that no one could mistake and which raised the alarm.

"You're bleeding," yelled Jacob "It's all over your dress."

Less bothered about my injuries than what was to follow, I scrambled to my feet and promptly passed out. In my deligate state, Jake received the blunt of maternal screams. I was taken to the hospital in Burnley for stitches. I have no idea how we got there. As far as I can recall, no one had a car. We must have gone by ambulance. I do remember being told that people all over Europe were injured because of Hitler's bombs, and I had taken up a doctor's time by disobeying my mother and harming myself. But I don't remember who said it to me. Surely not my mother. I paid the price for my disobedience with years of nightmares about falling through windows after being chased by Nazis.

These dreams alternated with others in which Rosa did not know we had moved and could not get in touch with us. The dreams continued long after letters from Rosa and my grandmother arrived at Rose Mount telling us they were safe. And then on one red-letter day, a note arrived announcing that Rosa was planning to make an extended visit to her sisters.

Aunt Alicia also found things to like about Rose Mount. These included John the coal man who lived next door. Actually, we all liked him because he was kind and gentle. He spent hours in the kitchen drinking cups of tea and chatting, mainly to Alicia, until his wife would yell at him that his supper was ready. He would stand up, take Alicia's hand, and kiss it in an old-fashioned manner. He then scurried across the two gardens to his own back door. Whatever the true nature of this curious relationship between a Jewish Londoner and a Methodist Lancastrian I never really knew, but we were never short of coal even at the height of the rationing.

I must have been an unhappy child. So unhappy, in fact, that I made a number of fruitless efforts to change my identity. I was always good at mimicry, so adopting a Rossendale accent was no problem to me. However, it greatly annoyed Alicia and my mother.

"For heavens sake child," they would say, "speak properly. You sound like a country bumpkin."

I didn't know what that was, but my new local accent was clearly disapproved of. So, I fell into the habit of switching accents between school and home, which seemed to keep everyone happy.

I also decided to change my date of birth. My best friend was named Hetty, a name I envied, as so many girls possessed it. She was born on the eighth of May. In order to seal our friendship and to avoid being the youngest in the class since my birthday was in September, I asked her one day, "Do you want to know a secret?"

"Yes," she eagerly replied.

"Promise not to tell anyone."

"I promise."

"My birthday is May eighth."

"It can't be," she said. "That's my birthday."

I may not have mentioned that Hetty was not the brightest girl in Crawshawbooth. "I know," I patiently replied. "But lots of people can be born on the same day. My sister Michaela was nearly born on the same day as our mother."

Hetty looked reflective, then she smiled. "That's good. We could be twins!" This was a situation I privately considered unlikely, but said nothing.

Then came the day that our teacher asked everyone to call out their birthday for the school register. I was in a state of terror. I couldn't lie and I dare not. Nor could I tell the truth with Hetty, all ears, sitting at the next desk. So I gestured to the teacher, who I considered to be a clone of the teacher who inflicted injustice with the cane, that I had a sore throat accompanied by a sudden loss of voice. I went up to her desk and whispered in her ear, "September the tenth Miss."

This teacher had made it clear that she did not care for evacuees of a certain origin. "Why," she demanded to know, "have you left your place? What's the matter child, cat got your tongue? There is nothing wrong with September tenth."

Except that it wasn't May eighth, thus making Hetty four months older than me.

"You told a lie," Hetty said to me at playtime. "That means you can't be my best friend."

"Alright," I replied. "I don't care." But I did. The only consolation was that I had already perceived that Hetty had a face like a pig and was a touch stupid.

Everyone else had a best friend except Brenda Dorphy, so I thought that I had better make do with her. Brenda was a real Catholic. She came from a big family and had a funny smell. The other kids said it was because she lived on a farm. She was only available as a best friend because of the smell and because she was said to have nits. I had asked Alicia what nits were to which she had merely replied, "God forbid you should ever know."

So I was none the wiser. It was a year later when a nurse known as "Nitty Norah" came to my junior school. Her duty was to grab everyone by the hair for an examination for nits and the dispensing of instructions to the parents of offending pupils. This is when I learned nits were the eggs of head lice. By which time, it was too late for me to assess whether Brenda Dorphy had been afflicted or not.

Brenda made pathetic attempts to win friends by bringing small trinkets beads or coloured glass bottles as bribes to school. She presented me with a pretty ring as a token of our newfound best friendship. It never occurred to me to ask where she got it, but I was uneasy enough not to show it to my mother or my aunt. Then one day, I was summoned to the office of the headmistress to join Brenda and her large rubicund mother who was in a state of agitation.

"Now Sophia," Miss Glass, the headmistress, said to me rather kindly, "I want you to tell me the truth. Brenda says you stole a ring from her that she had borrowed from her mother. What do you have to say?"

"I didn't," I whispered. "She gave it to me to show we were best friends."

"I didn't, liar! She took it from my desk. She wanted to sell it because she is a Jew," shrieked Brenda.

This was another occasion when, despite my resolve, the tears began to flow. I started to cry because I thought it was the ice slide story all over again. They wouldn't believe me.

"Don't cry," Miss Glass said gently "Just give the ring back to Mrs. Dorphy. There must have been a misunderstanding."

She put her arm around me and wiped my eyes with her handkerchief. She bid goodbye to Mrs. Dorphy as I handed her the ring that I had kept in the pocket of my navy blue gym knickers. To Brenda she said, "Go back to your classroom Brenda and please say nothing of this to anyone. Do you understand?"

Brenda simply nodded as she and her mother left seeming none too happy.

Miss Glass indicated that I should stay. "Don't worry my dear. I believe you. I did not like what Brenda said. But as my own Jewish father used to say to me, a child repeats what they hear at home and what they very often hear is a lot of ignorance. I am quite sure Brenda does not understand how upsetting what she said would be. Now sit here for a while until your eyes settle down. Then you can go back to class and say there has been a misunderstanding. I will explain it to your teacher."

Her words were intended to console and comfort me. Actually, they had the opposite effect. They made me feel guilty because the fact was that I had actually stolen something—not Mrs. Dorphy's ring, but something else. To Miss Glass's evident puzzlement, I started crying all over again. But I said nothing, and she did not ask.

I had stolen a stick of barley sugar that had been poking out of the pocket of a small green coat hanging on its peg outside our classroom. I had asked to leave the room to go to the toilets and saw it on my way out. It was so tempting. We did not see sweets in those times of austerity. Perhaps the child's mother had made it for him. Anyway, I took it out of the pocket and ran to the girls' toilets. Then I was too scared to eat it and upon hearing someone else coming into the lavatory, I panicked and threw it down the toilet pan.

I was not yet five years old and did not know how to handle situations like this. Should I make a clean breast of it or endeavour not to draw attention to myself? I approached the teacher and told her, "I saw a stick of barley sugar down the toilet." A small boy jumped up, "My mother made a barley sugar for my lunch. I left it in my coat pocket." He was allowed to leave the room to check if it was still there. He was back within seconds, wailing that it was no longer there. The teacher then marched the two of us to the girls' lavatories for me to show where I had seen it. They peered down the long funnel of the flush toilets and could see nothing.

The matter was reported to Miss Glass, the boy was instructed not to bring sweets to school again, and I was pronounced "a little romancer," which I accepted with relief. I knew being accused of fabricating a story was a whole lot better than being deemed a thief.

Almost all my memories of the early days of our exile, as I came to think of it, are painful but none more than those connected with my early schools. Looking back, I don't blame anyone except perhaps the government of the time. Many children already had bid farewell to their fathers as they were called to serve their country. The government tried to save the wartime children by hastily dispaching them to remote, presumed safe areas of the country. This usually involved separating children from their mothers in tearful scenes that children simply could not fully comprehend. Most often, the children were billeted with strangers, not all of whom were kind and generous.

The whole idea was full of good intentions and may, after all, have been the best that could be done. I was among the luckier ones since I was with my mother, baby sister, aunt, and cousin as well as 'Obbs and other determinedly cheerful Cockneys. Nevertheless, I was acutely aware of being different, an alien in a fairly comfortable but strange land. For those cast adrift with no one from their London lives, punished for misdemeanours they didn't know they had committed, made to eat unfamiliar food and correct their southern accents, it no doubt proved a trauma from which they never fully recovered. Some, we learned from 'Obbs, made life even more difficult for themselves by behaving very badly, pushing the tolerance and forbearance of their hosts to its limits.

So I have nothing to complain about in retrospect, though I thought I had plenty at the time. Nonetheless, I did not complain. I missed Rosa more than I could tell anyone for fear of upsetting my mother and Alicia who clearly made the best of the situation. I remember people remarking on what a good girl I was. This served to create an image I felt compelled to live up to most of the time. So a good deal of what I suffered, I kept to myself.

Chapter Five

Once, years later, when I hinted to my mother that my early school years were among the worst of my life, she was astonished. "But you were such a happy little girl," she said. And then she came out with a memory of her own. "Don't you remember that Rosa sent you what you called your Alice blue gown? You wore it for a concert at your second school."

Oh yes, I remembered it.

I remembered the dress arriving and my mother exclaiming that Rosa and Grandmother Stern must have spent all their clothing coupons on it. I even remembered the note of resentment in her voice as she said it. Rosa used to sing me a song about a girl in her "sweet little Alice blue gown, when I first wandered down into town" that ended with "I loved and I wore it, I'll always adore it, my sweet little Alice blue gown."

Now she had sent me a pale blue dress made of a kind of crepe material with a white-trimmed Peter Pan collar and a flared skirt beneath a white-trimmed belt. I did indeed adore it. I sniffed it for signs of Rosa's cigarette smell and my grandmother's essence of violet toilet water. I held it in front of me, then tried it on only to realize that my school socks and shoes were hardly the perfect accessories. But I knew they would have to do. I put the dress back in its wrappings and hid it under my bed.

My school held a concert in which I was to appear as a performer in a dance that was incomprehensible to me known as "Gathering Pea Cods." The dance was easy and I had readily mastered it. However, I had no idea what pea cods were, and I had not yet learned to ask questions. At the age of five, I preferred to pretend I knew what everyone else seemed to know. So I danced around and raised my hands to clap at the point where I presumed pea cods were being gathered.

"Don't you remember," my mother asked, "how you were the best dancer in your little blue dress that you loved so much and how Alicia, Jake, and I were in the audience and you waved at us happy as a lark?"

What I remember was that we had been told to ignore the audience. We were instructed to keep a fixed smile on our faces and, on no account, were we to wave to our parents. I was severely reprimanded for breaking the rules and "little show-off" was added to "romancer" in the list my teacher evidently was making of my negative characteristics. Even at age five, I recognized that neither label was totally inaccurate. My mother's summary at the end of our conversation about my miserable school days was, "Well, it doesn't seem to have done you any harm to look at you now."

She had a point. I was learning all the time, even if the process was sometimes painful. In my infants' school, we were required to spend what seemed to me a ridiculous and quite unacceptable amount of time playing with Plasticine. I thought it messy, smelly, and strictly limited in its possibilities.

I refused point blank to have anything to do with it. Each day, a monitor for each row of desks would distribute boards with fifty years of Plasticine stuck to them. Each board also had dollops of supposedly different colours of the smelly stuff with traces of all the other colours mixed in. I would instantly ask for a new stick of Plasticine, which came in flat-ridged pieces. I could then spend the lesson carefully separating the pieces. If no new sticks were available, I would while away the time scraping my board with a palette knife to see how clean I could get it before the bell rang.

The teacher put up with this rebellious behaviour for a limited time before expressing her exasperation, "If you continue to refuse to make Plasticine models like the rest of the class, you will have to spend playtime standing alone in the hall instead of going out to play."

As I actually preferred to stand alone in the hall to the nightmare of playtime outside in all weathers with no best friend, I replied, "Alright Miss."

After a few days of this routine, the teacher sent for my mother. For once, she was on my side or at least understood the futility of trying to change my mind. She explained to my teacher and Miss Glass that nothing would induce me to do things I saw no point in, especially if I also found them revolting. In the case of Plasticine, she could see my point. "Can't you find another activity for her while the others play with Plasticine?" she asked in my presence.

Miss Glass interceded again. The teacher did indeed introduce an alternative activity of cutting out coloured sticky paper shapes using a template and attaching them to a sheet of paper to form a picture.

This was offered to the entire class and clearly suited me much better. However, I did overhear my teacher refer to me as "a little madam" to one of her colleagues who came to the class and remarked in return that I was "a clever little madam."

I supposed "clever little madam" was rather better than "romancer" and "show-off" but something about the way it was pronounced made it sound like another bad thing. I remember thinking that I was a child who lacked approval outside my family, but I didn't mind. I knew I was different and that I was not to be blamed for it.

Even as a child, I had a strong faith in my own goodness despite my early school experiences. I credit Rosa for that, and I continue to thank her for it. A small child internalizes so much more than the surrounding adults realize. I believe that the psychologists are right in thinking that these early experiences shape our whole lives. I only quarrel with the common assumption that the results are inevitably negative.

About a year after I went to that school, things had quietened a bit in London. Rosa, who had never made it to Crawshawbooth, wrote to tell us they had all become quite used to sleeping in the Anderson shelter with the hollyhocks growing on the top of it to fool the Germans into thinking it was just a garden.

I remember my nights sleeping in the Anderson shelter before we were evacuated. To me there had been something of a fairy tale about sleeping there.

I connected the camouflaged shelter to Hans Christian Anderson whose stories Rosa had read to me. Then I remembered the nights I had spent huddled on a narrow bunk bed with Rosa in what had seemed a cosy heaven away from the bangs and crashes that were going on outside. I loved the smell of the paraffin lamp and the hushed tones of the adults all around me as I drifted off to sleep. In my bedroom, I was alone; but in the shelter, I was a safe, adored child surrounded by people who loved me.

Rosa's letter told us things were much better, and they were all managing fine. My father had insisted we stay in the north as, in his view, the war was far from ended. I never knew what made my mother obey him on this occasion but she certainly did. Aunt Alicia made the decision to return to London with Jake and to live in Grandmother Stern's house. I wondered why we didn't go, too.

John, the coal man left his wife and trailed after Alicia to London to become a paying lodger in my grandmother's house. My mother used to say that Alicia had gone home taking her Shabbas goy with her. But to my knowledge, John was never treated as anything other than a member of the family. I used to hear the adults say that John was waiting for Greg to fall under a bus. I thought that was a bit odd. Why would he do that? Anyway, fate had other plans. Greg managed to avoid street accidents and John died of a heart attack in Grandmother Stern's back bedroom, a lovesick goy for whom a whole family said kaddish.

So Miriam and her two little daughters were left alone in a house that was far too large for us. One day, the billeting officer came around and explained to my mother that we would have to move again to make room for a large family from Manchester. I have no recollection of how my mother felt about leaving Rose Mount and moving not far away into Sunny Bank, which was an even grander house where each family was allocated one large room.

To a six-year-old child, the place was a palace but one in which my mother, my baby sister, and I were confined

to one room. There were many rules about noise and running around and when each family, mostly from Manchester
was allowed to use the kitchen and bathrooms. I cannot say I
was any happier at Sunny Bank though it did have the secret
advantage of being closer to my derelict mill site than Rose
Mount had been.

Our room was dominated by a huge bed with wrought
iron head- and footboards and a lumpy mattress. The posts at
the four corners of the bed were topped by large knobs that
twisted off. I hid many a note to the deity inside those knobs.
I repeatedly wrote that it was time for the duration to end
so we could follow Alicia back to London. Whether anyone
ever found these notes, I shall never know. If someone did, it
is doubtful whether they would have been able to make out
a single word of my message except perhaps for my name
Sophia, which I had more or less perfected.

I shared the bed with my mother while Michaela slept in a
cot by my side of the bed. Miriam said that Michaela's sniff-
ing and snorting kept her awake. She wanted Michaela as
far away as possible, which wasn't far at all, but it seemed to
help and the noises did not bother me.

At night, my mother listened to programmes on the wireless such as *Palm Court Orchestra.* She also enjoyed *ITMA*
which she told me stood for "It's That Man Again"—someone called Tommy Handley, who made her laugh. This was
a rare enough event for me not to complain about being
kept awake. She laughed when an old woman came on and
said, "Can I do you now, Sir?" and the man kept saying, "I
don't mind if I do." This made my mother laugh like mad.
I suppose it was all 'double entendre' beyond the ken of a
six-year-old. But like the smells and muffled sounds of the
Anderson Shelter, these low-volume broadcasts my mother
liked to listen to pleased me and made me feel safe—unlike
the daylight and the strange world outside.

My father was away all this time "entertaining the troops"
as my grandmother would say with a sniff and a glance heav-
enward. I understood that my father's contribution to the war

effort was not to be put in the same bracket as that of my uncles who were in fighting units and risking their lives on a daily basis. Indeed, my mother's brother Joe was a prisoner of war in Italy. Years later, he told me that he developed a stomach ulcer due to scavenging and eating rotten food. But he would always add that it was nothing to what "the poor sods in Bergen Belsen had to suffer" and so he preferred not to talk about his experiences.

But my father was a hero as far as I was concerned—especially when he turned up one day at Sunny Bank with a miraculous toy he had made for me. It was a farmyard with all types of animals. These included some I considered a bit out of place on a farm, such as elephants and giraffes, but I loved them all the same. He had carved them for me out of bits of wood he had found in his camp when the troops were otherwise engaged. I was carried away with delight. I played with it for hours and improvised huts and fences from matchboxes and string. I adored my father and this gift; I guarded it with passion keeping it well away from Michaela's little fingers.

A few weeks later, my baby sister became very ill. She turned a bright red colour and was so hot her skin almost burned my fingers. The doctor, who looked after all the evacuees in Crawshawbooth, examined her and announced at once that she would have to be removed to an isolation hospital in Burnley. She had scarlet fever, which was a serious and highly infectious ailment in those days. Before he left to make the arrangements for Michaela's transfer to the hospital, he also gave me a thorough examination.

"This one's fit as a fiddle," he told my mother, "but she was probably the carrier." There was a bit of an epidemic in the local schools.

"Sophia always does that," my mother replied. "She's the one in school, so you would think she would be the one to get the fever. But she never gets anything while my poor baby is always ill."

What followed was, for me, the most terrible punishment brought about because I was perceived as the carrier of germs. The doctor ordered that all our toys and other things be burned. "This will stop the disease spreading to the other children in the house," he said.

"Not my farmyard!" I cried out.

"Everything," the doctor said. "I am afraid it is not worth the risk. I am sorry little lady, but your baby sister may have sucked those wooden animals and then you'd be the next victim. You wouldn't like that would you?"

It did no good to protest that I had never allowed baby Michaela to touch my farmyard or that I would rather have scarlet fever than lose it. It went into a big sack with all the other toys. These included my rag doll Suzy that Grandmother Stern had given me when we were evacuated. My Alfie Apple book given to me by the people in charge of the school where we had stayed when we were first "bombed out" in the blitzkrieg also went into the sack. My Alfie Apple book was my second favourite thing. It taught me there was something called a banana, in this case Bertie Banana, Alfie's friend. It was many more years before I encountered a banana in the flesh, as it were.

I didn't cry. I knew there was no point. I also knew my father would never make me another farmyard. He was definitely a one-off man. He went with us to see Michaela in the hospital. We had to look at her through a window because we were not allowed to go near her. As my grandmother said, "Thank God she made a complete recovery."

Michaela returned from the hospital with an expanded vocabulary. When people asked her if she felt better she would reply, "All gone," evidently referring to her fever. She said it a million times a day reminding me over and over that my farmyard was definitely all gone along with all our other toys.

I think this was the turning point for my decision that I was not a toy person. Indeed, I never asked for another toy until I wanted a two-wheeled bike like all my friends. My father gave me a foot-propelled scooter instead; this was probably all that he could afford. He passed it off by telling me,

"A scooter is much safer than a bike and more easily stored."

My father was quite a salesman.

"Thank you, Daddy." "I would really rather have the scooter," I lied. I think he believed me. Otherwise, I always asked for books that I hid from my siblings right up to the day I finally left home.

Chapter Six

The next thing I remember was being rehoused again. This house was allocated to us on the agreement that my mother would take in two evacuee children from Manchester. And so we moved away from Crawshawbooth to another district in Rossendale with a housing estate called Edgeside. This was situated on a hill above what amounted to a large village known as Waterfoot, with its own railway station long since closed down. It also had a cinema, The Kings, which became one of my favourite places, and a large grammar school.

For the time being, I was excited at the idea that we would have a private garden, and I would have my own bedroom. Even the idea of having other little girls moving in with us seemed promising. I drove my mother mad with questions about whether we were to spend the rest of the duration at Edgeside and whether there would be room for Rosa to come and stay with us. I also peppered her with less answerable questions, "Why is it called Edgeside? Can an edge have a side? Isn't an edge a side?"

As to Waterfoot—in time, why it was so named became more or less clear. At the head of one of the valleys that made up the Rossendale Valley was a hamlet called Water. From there the road led to Burnley, our nearest big town. At the other end of this valley was Waterfoot, which formed a T-junction with the road that stretched from Rawtenstall to Bacup, following the now defunct railway line which linked all the small towns and villages on either side of that reach of the Pennines with Manchester.

Marjorie and Ann, who moved into the house with us, came from Manchester.

To hear them talk, you'd think it was farther away than London. My mother told them firmly that it was not, but they were not convinced. They obviously felt as alien as we did, although the way they spoke was closer to the locals than ours.

It must have been difficult for them to be billeted with strangers and without their mother. It probably explained why they were so naughty and their stay was so short-lived. I never really knew how it came about, but before long, Marjorie and Ann had gone. They were replaced by a school friend of my mother's and her two little girls, Susan and Sheila. My mother caught me making a face when I learned Susan would be sharing my room. Susan turned out to be older and bigger than me and more than a bit bossy.

Mother admonished me, "You can't expect to have your own room when there's a war going on.

There are people being killed by the hundreds all over Europe, especially Jews. So we should thank our lucky stars that all we have to do is move up a bit to make room for people who are less fortunate and have been bombed out."

So I rather gracelessly welcomed Hilda Levy and her daughters mainly because she had been Rosa's best friend in school rather than my mother's who was in a class below them. Hilda Levy was her maiden name, which my family still used. Like my mother, she had also married a goy, in this case a complete goy not a half one. Hilda's husband, Walter Hubbard, was said by my family to be a five-foot weakling who had not been called up into the army due to his lung problems.

Apparently, he did war work in a factory, but Hilda pretended to everyone that he was engaged in some kind of intelligence work that was too secret to discuss. Only my family, including me, knew the truth. I knew it because I had eavesdropped on adult conversation, a habit my mother told me I ought to grow out of. On considering this remark, I decided I would grow out of it when I became an adult because then there would be no reason to eavesdrop. My mother also felt compelled to tell me in her strictest tones, "Sophia, you are not to mention anything about their father's weak lungs to Susan and Shelia."

I promised, but it turned out to be harder than I had imagined. Susan was quite horrible about my father being in the

Entertainment Corps and not doing dangerous and important things like her father. One day, her father turned up at
our house in civilian clothes, no doubt interpreted by his
girls and the neighbours alike as a clever device. Shortly
thereafter, the family was rehoused to a terraced house in
Loveclough, a little hamlet with a railway station. The small
village consisted solely of rows of homes and an evil-smell-
ing factory where Walter Hubbard continued his "secret war
work." Hilda was delivered of a son within a year of moving
to Loveclough. Her husband was diagnosed with tubercu-
losis and so, in the course of time, were two of his three
children.

We continued to see quite a lot of Hilda and her family.
The highlight of the visits, as far as I was concerned, was the
letters Hilda received from Rosa. They were written almost
as frequently as those that came to us, but these were written in a more general, less family-orientated way. Knowing
that Hilda read them to us, Rosa always sent a message and
kisses to me in these letters. I think I would have liked Hilda,
Rosa apart, with her long gorgeous, reddish, wavy hair. Kind
and gentle, she provided a calming influence on my mother
who tended to become excited about little things.

It was clear to me that my mother did not like Walter and
was glad to see the back of him. I did not entirely understand
one of the reasons at the time. I overheard my mother say
to a neighbour that Walter would go up to the bedroom and
then shout, "Hilda, I want you up here."

Years later, when understanding was beginning to dawn,
another piece was added to this jigsaw. "Men with TB are
known to be randy," Rosa wrote to my mother.

I guess that our move to Edgeside and a house of our own,
marked the beginning of continuous memories.

Our stay in that house long outlasted the time when I had
come to realize that the duration was nothing more than a
consoling phrase. I entered it at the age of seven and left it
when I went to university at seventeen. There was one brief
interlude when, under pressure from Rosa and Grandmother

Stern and daily cajoling by me, my mother agreed that I could go back to London for a while as long as I went to school.

Thrilled and somewhat nervous, to be travelling alone at age nine, I boarded the Yelloway coach that would take me to a new chapter in my life. At the end of a day's journey, we were in Kings Cross where Rosa met me for a joyous reunion. It was indescribably wonderful to be with Rosa and in my grandmother's house again. I was welcomed by the familiar smells of cholent that slowly cooked for the Shabbat lunch and the taste of my grandmother's bread pudding and chicken soup.

But the war was still raging. This was a time of V2 rockets, buzz bombs, and vivid memories. I saw what looked like a telegraph pole flying through the air. I was aware of a sudden cessation of the droning noise that came from the buzz bombs. This signalled an impending explosion. Everyone became silent trying to assess where it would hit. We did not breathe easily again until the bomb had found its mark and knew that, this time, it was not meant for us.

Did my family break the law by allowing me to return to London at this time when I was supposed to be evacuated? I didn't ask the question. In spite of the dangers, I was happy to be there.

But two things came along to change things and only one of them was sent by Hitler.

Chapter Seven

The air-raid warning had sounded in the middle of the night. I awoke to Rosa's picking me up out of my sleep, wrapping a blanket around me, and taking me down to the Anderson Shelter. It is odd, but the only recollection I have of Grandfather Stern is connected with this episode. He was already in the shelter, and I could see he was frightened. He must have died very shortly after this. I remember the explanation of his sudden death having something to do with his fear of leaving the shelter to use the lavatory. What could it have been? Urine poisoning? Is there such a thing? I evidently lacked curiosity about him and his abrupt disappearance.

However, memories of other events surrounding my return to London are clear. There were other adults in the shelter apart from Rosa and my grandparents. If they were all as frightened as my grandfather, I didn't notice it. Still sleepy, I was put to bed in one of the bunks. I was aware of the low voices discussing previous raids and where the bombs had fallen. One had landed next to the canal in the street behind my grandmother's house. Because it had destroyed most of the houses on that street, the residents on my grandmother's street became hosts to the surviving inhabitants—two or three of whom were now in the Anderson Shelter discussing the situation. Periodically, the conversation was interrupted by Rosa urging voices to be lowered. "Don't forget Sophia's here," she said. "She doesn't need to know what's going on."

I must have fallen asleep, lulled by the whispering of the adults and the puttering of oil lamps. From time to time, I was roused by someone temporarily leaving the shelter to take stock of the situation and then report back. The women made tea on the paraffin stove, discussed how long before the all-clear would sound, and how long they could go without a cigarette. When the air raid sirens sounded the all-clear, I didn't hear it. When Rosa woke me it was broad daylight and all the neighbours had left. "Time to get up for school," Rosa said. "Breakfast is ready in the kitchen."

My grandmother's house had something called a scullery where all the cooking and clearing up took place. Another room, called the kitchen, was where we ate, listened to the wireless, and people gathered to talk. Topics of conversation centred on who had been bombed, who had received letters from their husbands or sons, and what was happening to the Jews. I liked the kitchen with its open fire, the wireless set high up on a shelf that was covered by a velvety green table-cloth with tassels. I loved the feel of this cloth as I ran my hand over its surface and tried to untangle the tassels one from the other.

I enjoyed being the only child with all the grown-ups and listening to their stories. Once, before we were all sent away, my grandmother gave a birthday party in that very room for my cousin Jake when he was two.

That was the first time I had ever had a balloon. Jake wanted mine because it was red. Despite Rosa's entreaties that it was his birthday, I refused to swap. But when my red balloon burst, I wanted Jake's, who happily gave it to me. Looking back on this, I don't remember feeling guilty.

War or no war, I had to attend school. Rosa had enrolled me in Oliver Goldsmith's Junior School, a fifteen-minute walk that I was not allowed to do on my own. The people who lived next door to my grandmother had left London to live with relatives in Canada. Aunt Alicia had rented the house for her and Jake until Uncle Greg returned from the war and they could find a place of their own. She wanted to be near Rosa and my grandmother (and possibly "poor John"), so either she or Rosa would walk me to school.

One day, we were just about to set out when the air-raid siren sounded again. Alicia, Jake, Rosa, and I were in the kitchen. My grandmother was upstairs making beds. "You take the kids down to the shelter," Rosa said to Alicia. "I'll get Mum."

Alicia shepherded Jake and me down the passage, through the scullery, and out to the garden heading for the Anderson Shelter. "I want to wee," Jake yelled.

There was an outside toilet next to the scullery. It had a wooden seat like a bench with the lavatory bowl set in the middle. My grandmother always scrubbed that wood until it was practically white and hung sheets of newspaper with a string from a hook in the wall, which we were to use as toilet paper as part of our war effort. As Alicia was taking Jake into the lavatory, she said to me, "You go on down the shelter, there's a good girl."

At that moment, we heard a sound that made Alicia freeze. "It's a buzz bomb," she called out to me. "Go, go. Come on Jake. You'll have to wee in the pot."

I heard the drone of the missile coming nearer as we went down the steps into the shelter. Alicia stopped at the top of the steps. "Mum, Rosa," she shouted. "Quick. Come down. Hurry."

As Rosa appeared at the door to the garden, the buzzing noise stopped. Rosa screamed, "Mum, Mum." Alicia ran and dragged Rosa to the shelter, pushing Jake's head and mine down inside as she pulled her sister in after her. The silence was shattered by an enormous explosion and the sound of breaking glass.

"I've got to get Mum," Rosa shouted as she pushed Alicia aside and scrambled up the steps of the shelter.

In the distance, I could hear a cry coming from the house. Alicia's face turned a scary white. Before she followed her sister, she firmly stated, "Stay where you are. Don't move. Do you hear me?" Minutes later, Jake and I heard the all clear but stayed where we were.

"The windows have blown in," I heard Rosa shouting. "Mum's got glass in her eyes. We have to get an ambulance."

Jake started to cry. I put my arm round him.

"I think Nanny's okay," I said. "But she's hurt. We'd better stay here." I found some biscuits in the little storage cupboard in the shelter and gave some to Jake to make him stop crying.

It seemed ages before we heard the bell of an ambulance. Alicia came back to us and said,

"It's okay to come out now. Everything's a bit of a mess so mind where you step. Nanny has to go to the hospital to have some glass removed from her eyes. The bomb fell down the street. A lot of houses have been ruined but ours is fine except for the windows."

"What about the people?" I asked her.

"We don't know, love. But the ambulances came quickly. One of them is taking Nanny to Moorfields. She'll be alright, don't worry."

But she wasn't. She was in the hospital a long time and when she came home she couldn't see. She pretended to us that she could. "You know I've always told you I have eyes in the back of my head," she laughed when Jake asked her if she could see. He looked at the back of her head, but I turned away so she wouldn't know I was crying. Then I cried more because I knew she couldn't see me crying.

But she knew anyway and said, "Don't cry, Sophia.

Hitler took my eyes, but he didn't take my sixth sense children. You'll see how much your old Nanny knows what's going on, eyes or no eyes." In the short term, this meant many hospital visits, but nothing could be done to restore her sight. Despite the injury, she refused to leave London.

Rosa had been drafted to work for the war effort and soldered biscuit tins in Peek Freans biscuit factory for the troops. That was one of the reasons I had to return to Edgeside and my mother. The other reason was only loosely connected to the war. Between air raids and my grandmother's visits to the hospital, Alicia made sure I attended school where attendance, mine included, was patchy to say the least. No doubt for that reason, I remember very little about it except that the building was large and on a main road. Farther along that same road, there was an Odeon cinema that had been bombed during a Saturday morning children's matinee. A large, famous department store suffered a similar fate that included looting by the local citizenry. The looting shocked my family more than the damage done by the German bombs.

No doubt these events and many similar daily occurrences explained why I attended school in an atmosphere characterized by extreme nervousness. It may even explain why, one morning in school assembly, I was violently sick. Fortunately, I was standing at the end of a row so I vomited only on the floor. Nevertheless, the children near me stepped back in disgust, and no teacher made any attempt to come to my aid. Of course, I should have left the hall to make for the toilet, but I was frozen to the spot feeling embarrassed on top of feeling faint. Through my fog of distress I heard the headmistress' voice booming out, "Get out you disgusting child."

I never returned to that school. But I did develop a paranoia about throwing up in public places. When it was finally determined that I must return to my mother, I pleaded with her not to make me go to school. She had no choice. She enrolled me in the local junior school in Waterfoot where she spoke to the Headmistress and my class teacher about my problem. The result was that I was allowed to stand at the end of a row nearest the toilet in assembly with permission to go out if ever I should feel sick. I never did, but it was many years before my fear of vomiting in public left me. When a certain American president threw up at a formal dinner in Japan years later, no one in the world could have had more sympathy for him than I did.

Chapter Eight

The house in Edgeside was a small, semi-detached three-bedroom council accommodation. The houses were built in rows on the side of a hill. The pavements were higher than the entrances, which were reached by a flight of stone steps leading down to the front door.

The house was oddly arranged with the kitchen at the front, and it was the only room on the ground floor in line with the front door. The kitchen looked out on a steeply sloping garden—in our case, full of foot-high weeds. After my father returned from the war, and especially during his lengthy resting periods, he made half-hearted attempts to improve the gardens at both the front and the back of the house, which included quite an expanse of lawn. But as long as my parents lived there—and it must have been all of twelve years—the gardens were never anything but a mess. My mother, a compulsively orderly housewife, was simply not interested in anything beyond the walls of the house. And my father was easily discouraged.

It must have bothered me a bit to live in the only house in the avenue that did not have manicured lawns, herbaceous borders with hues that changed with the seasons, and neatly clipped hedges. I say this as to this day, I dream of looking out onto the wilderness and planning how I would deal with it. However, it must be said that the jungle of weeds, unfinished rockery, paths that led nowhere, and foot-high pampas grass that made up the garden of the Rosen household was the neighbourhood children's favourite playground, not approved of by their mothers.

Grass snakes appreciated the natural surroundings, as did a hedgehog that my mother, who was as indifferent to domestic animals as she was to the garden, took a fancy to. "I'll call him Henry," she announced. She fed him bread and milk, as if that were what he was thoroughly used to, and referred to him in terms more appropriate to a secret lover. "Come on my darling. Breakfast is ready. Wasn't that a lovely breakfast I made for you?"

Anyway, Henry thrived on this love and attention even surviving a winter's hibernation in his homemade nest in the coal shed. Thereafter, Henry became my father's excuse for never cutting the grass.

Actually, the best effort made at tackling our garden was by a certain Mr. Hawkins, the insurance man, who called on us every week to collect our contributions. It was clear to me that he fancied my mother who, to my mind, did nothing to discourage him. He seemed to spend more time in our house than in the house next door—no doubt because he was not offered tea and cake there. One upshot was that he offered to come on the weekend to scythe the lawn. He was as good as his word and for a few weeks our lawn looked quite respectable. I don't think anything of significance ever happened between Mr. Hawkins and my mother; however, both his prolonged visits and his gardening stopped when my father appeared on the scene. I was glad. My mother had observed my lack of warmth toward Mr. Hawkins. "You don't like Mr. Hawkins do you Sophia? He has been so kind to us. Why should you not like him?"

"Because he's boring," I replied "and he smells of damp."

All the avenues of the estate were built one above the other on the hillside linked by steep brews or hills. During the winters, these became natural sledge runs. Our house was on the corner of one of these brews, so I was awakened every morning by the sound of workers' clogs as they made their way down to the cotton mills in the valley below. During the war time days, it was mostly the older men and some women who worked the mills between 6:30 a.m. and 7:30 p.m. every weekday. An aerial photograph would have captured hundreds of people descending on foot from the hills on either side of the valley to the mills below. Opposite Edgeside was a large hill called Seat Naze. This was a plateau that included the village of Newchurch and beyond that, as the crow flies, the market town of Rawtenstall. It was rather splendid, rather wild Penine country, close to Pendle Hill of Lancashire Witches fame, but its charm eluded me. To me, it appeared cold and hostile. It was simply not where I belonged or wanted to be. It was clear to me that my mother shared my feelings or, perhaps, it was she who had transferred them to me.

Looking back, I recognize that the house in Edgeside was the most stable home the family ever had. Twelve years was a long time in the life of the Rosens. The steep stone steps that led down to the front door were bounded by a precarious wooden railing. A cracked and broken path led around the side of the house to the back door, our daily entrance. The path oozed tar in the summer, which my father called the "black stuff." My mother, however, called it "the bane of her life" because on the few days each year that were hot enough to melt it, one or the other of us trod in it and trailed it in the house. Even what my grandmother called "elbow grease" was unable to remove it. The only people known never to bring tar into the house were the ambulance men because they were the only people to use the front door.

Dock leaves grew to the height of the front steps and long, skin-cutting grass bordered the path. Through this jungle, we could see the steps next door and the neatly trimmed lawns and proper flowers. There were no walls or fences between any of the houses. The children could run across the front of the whole block until they came to the Rosen's house. At this point, they might hesitate fearful of getting their arms cut to shreds and dock leaf marks on their clothes, which was enough to drive their mothers wild.

Three steps led up to the back door that opened with a latch leading into a short passage. The loo was on the immediate left and the coal house was next to it. A row of pegs for our outdoor clothes lined the wall on the right. This was also the area where we had to leave our muddy wellies. At the end of this passage, another latched door led into the kitchen. I do not remember the passage with any affection. It was a cold and frequently smelly place with tiny bits of coal on the floor. It was totally unlike Grandmother Stern's passage back in London. Her passage was warm, smelled of the paraffin stove, and had green and white patterned lino all the way from the front door that everyone used to get to the scullery.

Even in winter, our kitchen was the only room in the house which was almost never cold. It housed a gas-fired copper for boiling up the laundry, which always seemed to be on the go. Like the house in Stoneholme terrace, it had a stone-flagged floor that my mother covered with rugs made out of bits of cloth. These rag rugs were made by a local lady we called Auntie May.

I suppose the kitchen had all the usual things such as a stove, table, and chairs, but the only other feature I remember clearly was a pulley for drying the washing. This was attached to the ceiling and was hauled up and down with a rope. This allowed my mother to dry the clothes on wet days when she could not put them out on the clothesline and to air them after they had been ironed.

I don't have happy memories of the pulley. My mother changed the bed linen on Mondays and spent all day washing it in the copper, ringing it out, and hanging it on the pulley. When I came home from school, she was worn out and the place smelled of wet washing with condensation everywhere. More dismaying was that my poor mother had had no time to do anything else except chat with Mr. Hawkins for Monday was also his day for contributions. This meant that I had to make the beds and do some dusting before I could get on with reading the *Girl's Crystal* or my homework.

The best thing about the kitchen was the larder. Every home had a pulley and a larder. The larder was a small room at the back of the kitchen and under the stairs. This was a cool area where the food was kept. Only the wealthy had refrigerators. As no food lasted long in our household and very little was left over, the larder served very well—especially in view of the habitually arctic weather. Perishable goods were kept on a stone slab at the back of the larder and on packets and tins on shelves that ran the length of the wall.

When my father came home from the army, he made a wooden bread bin to go under the stone slab. He explained as he worked, "It has to have air holes to allow the bread to breathe. It is the same with cheese." I found these facts of life intriguing at the time and still have never forgotten them.

There were days, especially before the war ended, when there was not much in the larder at all. I remember eating condensed milk on bread and reconstituted egg powder; my mother never allowed us to go hungry. Mr. Hawkins sometimes let her off paying the insurance money, and our neighbours, the Woodstocks, were good to us. Because their dad had TB, he didn't have to go in the army. His job as a bus conductor must have been quite good because his wife used to say, as I overheard in one of my eavesdropping sessions, "We always have a bit left over at the end of the week."

Chapter Nine

By the time my sister Miranda was six and my brother Sean four, we had lived in Edgeside for about seven years and were almost accepted as locals. We even managed to gain some notoriety when our kitchen appeared in the local press. Sean had climbed into the copper and couldn't get out—his legs were stuck around the paddles.

From the telephone kiosk, Mrs. Woodstock called the fire brigade to get him out. So I suppose they were responsible for notifying the press who sent a photographer to take pictures of Sean stuck in the copper. He was pretty upset at the time. As he couldn't hold it any longer, he peed in the copper. But you wouldn't know that from the photo. After it was published, he forgot all about the pain and the embarrassment and took it to his infant school to show the teacher.

Later, he made a scrapbook entitled "Important Events in the Life of Sean Rosen." This began with the photograph of him in the copper surrounded by firemen. Subsequent photos included the various times he had a plaster cast on an arm, a leg, or a foot. The numerous accidents he suffered as a boy were well documented.

A door from the kitchen led into the living room, which was an apt description for how the room was used. This was where my mother knitted, sewed, fed the baby, and ironed. She also cooked in an oven heated by a coal fire set in a huge black grate. This was the room where we kept the radio, our books, and, in a series of wall cupboards labelled on the inside with our names, our personal possessions. It was also where I did my homework and painted (I once got ten out of ten for painting the scene in our living room). We played Ludo, Snakes and Ladders, and Scrabble in this room. The baby lay in its pram while we entertained friends. On Friday nights and Sunday lunches, we ate our meals in the living room. The rest of the time, we ate in the kitchen.

The focus of the room was the grate that had to be cleaned and black leaded once a week. It was surrounded by a high fire guard with a brass top that my mother polished until its reflection danced on the ceiling. When we had coal, the fire was a very efficient means of heating. My mother became an expert at gauging its temperature so that she could use the oven to warm food without spoiling it and to make her delicious cakes that she concocted without using scales.

But coal was rationed, and "Poor John" had gone to London. I could never make up my mind which I hated most—the cold days when we had no coal or those when we did and I had to make the fire. I used to go downstairs on cold December days and stare at the grate with loathing. Today, these installations are collectors' items sold by shops such as "Amazing Grates" and "Grate Fires of London." But when I was a child, I perceived these grates as difficult and demanding beasts. The black leading and the cleaning aside, it was a difficult job to get them lit. First, the ashes from the night before had to be cleaned out. Next, I rolled up newspaper, not too tight, to act as tinder. Finally, I stuck in bits of wood and fire lighter before topping it off with small pieces of coal. Only then would I set the paper alight with a match. If I was lucky, it worked. If the wood, which was bought in bundles for three pennies, was not absolutely dry, it would smoulder and the fire went out. It was a disaster if the fire refused to light. With the cold weather, the stone floors, and the wet washing, icicles would form on the inside of the windows when there was no fire.

One day, after three attempts, I failed to get the fire going. My recourse was to pretend I had fainted, so everyone would feel sorry for me. My father was not around to help. It must have been one of the few occasions when he had a booking away from home. My mother fetched Albert Woodstock from next door. He was a bus conductor and not trained in first aid, but he had two cross-eyed daughters who were always fainting—presumably because of focus and balance problems. He had experience, but I fooled him.

He announced, "She has probably been affected by the fumes from the firelighters. Maybe you should excuse her from fire-lighting duties for a bit."

I also have a memory about that fire that is linked to our cat named Bill. My mother hated domestic animals, and I cannot imagine why we were allowed to keep Bill. Maybe he just turned up like the hedgehog, and she hadn't the heart to throw him out.

Bill the cat and my little sister Michaela, who was the baby at the time, were best friends. She treated him like a doll and dressed him up in her old clothes before wheeling him around in her doll's pram. Bill tolerated this attention in a most unnatural way.

One day, I ran to my mother in alarm and announced, "There is a funny smell coming from the oven next to the fire." The fire was roaring and giving out a prodigious amount of heat. My mother sniffed the air and hurriedly opened the oven door. Bill the cat staggered out howling in anguish.

"How on earth did he get in there?" my mother demanded.

At the time, Michaela called herself, "Baby." In her childish manner, she lisped, "Baby put Bill in oven to dry after his bath, now naughty Bill all hot." The poor steaming cat jumped into the arms of his tormentor for comfort.

My mother, won over as usual by Michaela's charm, scowled at me, "You should have kept a better eye on your sister," she said. It's no wonder I hated that fire.

Sean, however, saw the necessity of fires as an entrepreneurial opportunity. He canvassed the neighbourhood asking the residents for their old wood. He then chopped up the wood, bundled it, and sold it back to the neighbours for two-and-a-half pennies.

Our living room had two large windows that gave a generous view of the wilderness beyond. It was edged on all sides by the horticultural triumphs of the Woodstocks at number 50, the Howards at number 54, and the Ashworths opposite, whose house was in the avenue below ours. The Ashworth's garden backed onto ours. Mr. Ashworth was forever spraying stuff at it—apparently to stop it being infected from the Rosen's garden.

My memories of Sunday mornings in Edgeside are of church bells and the sound of manually operated lawn mowers and hedge clippers. It was irritating, but I took comfort in the fact that the Woodstock girls were cross-eyed, the Howard's father was always drunk when he wasn't mowing the lawn, and the Ashworth's daughters all had lice. I had become aware of this fact when standing behind one of the daughters in school assembly and witnessing the horror of lice parading up the parting of her pigtailed hair.

The cupboards in the lounge, where we each had our own section bearing our name, provided their own vivid memories too. Because of the dampness, green mould grew on the inside of the cupboards. Once a year, we had to remove our things and put them "somewhere safe" as part of my mother's general spring-cleaning event. I can vividly recall the smell of disinfectant. My mother's instructions to put our belongings somewhere safe were a joke because there was nowhere safe. During these annual clean-outs, I discovered that things I had confined to the cupboard, which had no lock, were no longer there.

"One of you has been stealing my things," I accused my siblings in general.

"Who wants your rotten things?" Michaela sniped.

"What things?" Miranda asked in innocence.

"Not me," Sean piped up.

"You should be more careful with your things," Mother responded.

Once again, left to my own devices, I designed my own safe. I found a loose floor board in the bathroom. This was a perfect place to secrete letters from my father that included theatre programmes from the Hippodrome New Brighton and other places where he appeared. I added school work for which I had received ten out of ten, "excellent, well done," and bits of my mother's own recipe fudge wrapped in toilet paper. I was a natural hoarder but saving the fudge just didn't work. My siblings ate theirs when it was fresh. I threw mine away after I had tried to lick off all the bits of toilet paper that had stuck to it.

The front of the house offered the smallest of lobbies that was not even large enough for an umbrella stand. The small area was bounded by a door to the lounge on one side and the front door of the house on the other. This was the front door only ever used by the ambulance men who were called to take Sean off to have stitches or medical attention after one of his many accidents.

A steep flight of stairs led to the bedrooms and bathroom. This was a strange and somewhat awkward arrangement, but I don't think any of us questioned it at the time. Architectural idiosyncrasies were not topics frequently discussed at the Rosen dinner table, but I did wonder what kind of planner decided that a staircase should be placed in the front of the house.

As long as we lived in that house, the stairs were never carpeted or covered with linoleum. My father had a go at varnishing the steps a dark brown at each side and a lighter brown in the middle to give, in his dreams, the effect of a central runner of carpet. The result was disastrous. Everything stuck to the varnish including Bill the cat. In any case, my father was fed up by the time he reached the top of the main flight—the steps that turned to the bedrooms were never varnished.

"Better they had all been left like that," my mother complained. "They would have been easier to clean."

I remember the stairs seemed to have a life of their own. They creaked. I mean they creaked all on their own without anyone treading on them. My bedroom was at the top of the stairs and on the right. I used to lie in my bed convinced that someone had broken into the house using the front door. My parents would be unaware of these telltale sounds because they were listening to *Book at Bedtime* on the radio and drinking their cocoa. It was unlikely that they would suspect anyone coming through the front door because no one ever did.

This provided me with little solace, and I heard the same noises every night. No rapist or burglar or any other class of villain who wished me harm could be clever enough to replicate those noises so exactly that I would be taken by surprise. But I could never convince myself that these were the normal creaks. It always took me ages to fall asleep.

The upstairs was home to three bedrooms plus a tiny, extremely chilly bathroom that was sited at the front of the house by the aforesaid mad architect. In the beginning, when we first moved to Edgeside, the largest bedroom had been assigned to the evacuees from Manchester. Michaela and I were given the second largest bedroom, and Mother used the smallest bedroom. Over the years, these arrangements changed as the household became progressively more crowded. All the girls were squashed into the largest room. Sean, the only boy, had the smallest bedroom to himself, and my parents took over the middle-sized room.

The only thing that did not change was the temperature, which was unceasingly cold. No one wanted to leave his or her warm bed in the morning, and everyone tried to avoid bed-making duty. The bathroom was torture by freezing. My father would never allow any type of heater in there.

Whenever the topic was raised, he would remind us of an experience during his touring days.

"When I was on the road with a repertory company, we stayed in cheap digs. Our bathroom isn't even cold compared to those where we stayed. One of the young actresses balanced an electric fire on the end of the bath to keep herself warm. Of course, it fell in the water and electrocuted her. Instead of being stone cold she was stone dead."

Eli was not a bit amused when we all joined in with the last line since we knew the script by heart.

So we all preferred, at least while we were still of an age when bottoms were rude, but not taboo, to stand in the stone sink in the kitchen to be bathed by our mother. I can hear her saying,

"Up as far as possible, down as far as possible, and then finally dealing with possible," as she used to say.

The awkward entrance, the obstinate fires, the steep squeaky stairs, and the lack of privacy was my family home. It was never really comfortable. Often there was a row going on between my parents about money, my father's work, or lack of it, and ultimately about whether or not I should be allowed to go to university. My mother was against it saying she needed my help and the money I could earn. My father thought money was never of first importance, hence all the rows. Invariably on my side, he favoured my attending university. He was backed by Rosa, of course, my grandmother, and my English teacher. Gradually, they wore my mother down. I never held her opposition against her. She simply did not understand why I should want to leave home and go to university.

I know she had always considered me strange, "More Rosa's child than mine," as she proclaimed to my father.

I even considered myself a bit strange or it may be more accurate to say "not the same as the others."

This created a distance between us. Rosa did not consider me strange, so why did my mother? I loved my mother and always understood that she was doing the best she could. I also realized my relationship with my mother was not as meaningful to me as my relationship with Rosa.

This was confirmed when I saw my mother and Michaela together. Michaela was her daughter in a way that I was not. They were soul mates who shared tastes, temperament, and attitudes while I watched puzzled from the sidelines.

My poor mother's life was one long struggle with poverty, loneliness, alienation, and the disappointment at how her life had turned out. She never seemed to be where she belonged and, in fact, for much of her life this was exactly the situation. I was aware, of course, that she did not understand and was not much interested in what was going on in my young life; therefore, I never bothered to tell her. I honestly cannot remember one long, significant conversation with her. She was always busy, always preoccupied, and almost always unhappy. My main endeavour was to be careful not to add to her troubles.

There were tender moments. I remember she let me feel her tummy when she was expecting Sean and allowed me to comb her long brown hair to style it into all kinds of patterns. Sometimes she baked one of her special apple pies for me and saved the pastry flowers from the top just for me. Other times, she would tell me about the book she was reading. Before my father came home from the war, she occasionally allowed me to stay up late to listen to *Book at Bedtime* with her. But mostly, our relations were not close. It was many years and another kind of life before I learned that she had any words for me other than "strange."

School was the one arena in which I could be different to good effect. School, once I had passed the infants stage, was my spiritual home. Once I was over the fear of vomiting in assembly, I looked forward to school days more than to weekends and holidays. I was driven by the need to get ten out of ten in everything. I strove to be top of the class across the board and to be good at sports. I succeeded. It wasn't important whether or not my achievements made me unpopular. This was my one way of being special, even superior, and I enjoyed it.

I may have been only a temporary resident in Rossendale whose mother spoke funny and whose father had nothing to do with the mills. We might have been classified as evacuees though the war was well over. Most evacuees had left and "good riddance." We didn't go to church, and my family was a mixture of Jew and Red Neck (Catholic); but I was clever. I was perfectly aware that "clever" was not considered an altogether good thing, but it earned me a certain respect. Some teachers were grudging about it, others kind and encouraging. In those classes, the kids called me "teachers pet" which, whatever the intention, had the effect of making me feel protected.

Oddly enough, I was never aware of what I would later describe as anti-Semitism. Jews, even during the time of the evacuations from London and Manchester, were sparse. I suppose few people in our bit of northeast Lancashire had any idea what it meant to be a Jew. We knew a few Jewish families. They had *schmatter* (clothes and fabric) stalls in Rawtenstall market, but they lived in Burnley or Accrington. One family of tailors had a shop in Waterfoot. Their son Michael was a bit older than me, but we were in the same junior school.

Michael once got in a fight because he took exception when he heard someone say they had been "jewed." The result entailed both of us being summoned to the headmaster's office. He explained to us,

"No offence was intended by the child who had used that phrase. It is simply a local phrase meaning someone has been cheated and people don't mean to say that Jews are cheats. It is just a phrase handed down from father to son. You should not be upset by it."

Michael appeared to accept this explanation as some class of apology but I ventured,

"Shouldn't it be stopped?"

"I think my dear," the headmaster replied, "that trying to stop it might do more harm than good." This response left me to try to figure out what he meant. By the time I went to grammar school at age eleven, Michael's family and their shop had left Rossendale. The Eli Rosen family may have been the one surviving specimen of a Jewish-Catholic family in the area. I seemed determined to justify the pronouncements of all those who claimed that such people are too clever by half.

Because we were poor, we never went anywhere for what the other kids called "us holidays." We spent the long, summer holiday from school going for walks on Seat Naze, or fishing for tiddlers at Jack Lodge, a local pond. A rare treat was accompanying my father for a one-night gig.

The summer before I turned eight in the September, my sister Miranda was born. This gave me something to write about in the inevitable post-vacation essay upon our return to school. "What I did in the summer holidays" was always a problem for me. The whole of Rossendale went to Blackpool or Scarborough. For families who were a bit better off, they might head to Morecambe or Southport for what was called "Wakes Week." I always thought this to be an odd title since it lasted a fortnight during which the valley went into a deep sleep. My classmates would produce essays about beaches and piers and what they brought back for their Grandma.

Chapter Ten

When class reassembled in the school term that would see my ninth birthday, I made a decision. I could not possibly write another essay describing my holiday walking in the hills and catching tiddlers. During the holidays, I went with my mother to the cinema to see *Road to Alaska* with Bing Crosby, Bob Hope, and Dorothy Lamour. Completely enchanted, I begged my mother to let us see it again. She relented and we saw it again before the end of that week. The rest of my holiday was spent reading everything available in the children's section of the Rawtenstall library on Alaska and other Arctic countries.

It was only natural that my "What I did in the summer holidays" essay described in minute detail how the entire Rosen family ventured to Alaska. I described baby Miranda as swaddled in seal skin while the family had crisscrossed Alaska in a sledge drawn by a team of six huskies. Although Eli Rosen had not yet made a permanent return from the army, he learned to handle the sledge with consummate skill.

As I had never been on either a ship or a plane, I was necessarily vague about how we got to Alaska. However, I made up for this omission by inserting bits of authentic Alaskan dialogue into the narrative as well as amazing anecdotes based on the adventures of Messrs. Crosby and Co.

That year, my teacher was a very short, former naval officer named Archie Thistlethwaite who possessed a strong line in sarcasm and a "penchant" for little girls. At one time, he asked my mother's permission to take me to the museum in Burnley and to the cinema afterward. With an instinct beyond my years, I hoped she would refuse. However, she seemed flattered and had agreed I could go. Nothing happened on the outing, but I instinctively felt his interest in me was not healthy. I subsequently asked my mother not to let me go out with him again. She immediately became suspicious and asked me whether Mr. Thistlethwaite "had touched me or anything." I assured her he had not. I just didn't want to be with him again. From then on, my mother became rather aggressively watchful.

Whether Mr. Thistlethwaite detected this, along with my new reserve, or not, the fact is that he took particular delight in directing his sarcasm at me thereafter. My essay on "Our Holiday in Alaska" gave him a good opportunity to practice this gift.

"Well children," he announced, "the most interesting and, might I say, unusual holiday this year was enjoyed by the Rosen family. They went on a holiday with the stars to Alaska. Sophia, will you please tell us all about how your family got there, where you stayed, and how you managed to cover the entire frozen north in just two weeks?"

A sensitive man would have realized why I had made up such a colossal lie. Mr. Thistlethwaite, however, belonged to the breed of teacher that takes particular pleasure in tormenting a child either to raise a laugh or to reduce his child victim to tears.

Naturally, I wanted to cry, but I was determined that I would not. On the spot, I decided that the only thing to do was to tell the class that I had made the story up for two reasons. First, I did not know that the essay had to be factual. Secondly, I did not want to write about my real holiday which had been rather boring. I explained that I had read about Alaska and seen *Road to Alaska* twice with my mother. Emboldened, I continued by saying that if Mr. Thistlethwaite would agree, I would read my essay aloud if the class wanted to hear it. I received resounding affirmation from the class, so the discomforted teacher had no choice but to let me read. He never forced his attentions on me again.

The recitation of my fictional holiday in Alaska had another unanticipated result. It won me the admiration of a classmate named Glenda. I had coveted her friendship, but she had been the best friend of the extremely possessive and pugnacious Antonine. Blonde, blue-eyed, rather plump, and very good-natured, Glenda was the type of student who frequently is popular in school. Her family was rather well-off as attested by the clothes she wore and the rationed sweets she always seemed to have. In retrospect, Glenda was a rather bovine, uninteresting child, but she certainly was never short of a best friend.

When she linked arms with me following the Alaska episode and led me out to the playground in a way normally reserved for Antonine, a reaction from that quarter was quick to follow. I found a note on my desk after the break that read: "Scool yard. Afternun playtime. Chuse a second." Pugnacious Antonine was not the most literate child in the class. I had no need to guess the author. One look across the desk at the scowl on her face said it all.

I had been in the school long enough to learn its code of honour. Summoning someone to a fight backed up by a second was the customary practice—a throwback to duelling. I knew I would have to present myself that afternoon or be labelled "cowardy custard" for the rest of my school days. I didn't want to fight for the simple reason that I didn't think I would win. But my own sense of honour would not allow me to ignore Antonine's challenge.

I chose a boy to be my second and we duly presented ourselves at the appointed time and place. No Antonine. She avoided my eyes when we reassembled in class, but I turned up on the playground with my second every afternoon for the rest of the week. Still no Antonine. I had won. My second was a disappointed man, telling me I had only won on a technicality. As far as I was concerned, it was the best way. I was small, nervous, and different, but my stock in the class went up.

Glenda and I remained friends for some years after we went to separate secondary schools. She was never going to be the brain of Britain, but she was a good soul and I valued her sweet nature and generosity—as well as her sweets. If truth be told, I also valued her continued admiration of me and my scholastic achievements. She was a girl completely without jealousy or resentment and genuinely rejoiced in the successes of others.

Chapter Eleven

Whatever my satisfaction with my school life, it was nothing compared to the happiness I experienced on the return of my father from the war. It occurred in the same year as our holiday in Alaska, the year before my brother Sean was born. I had always had a special love for my father. It was not the same as my devotion to my Aunt Rosa largely because it was based on mythology rather than actual contact.

My father had been an absentee figure for most of my life. No doubt part of my special feeling arose from a sense of defiance against the antipathy he provoked in Rosa and my grandmother. It was clear that they disapproved of him—somehow he had disappointed my mother. But in my mind, he was invested with a kind of romanticism. A striking looking actor, he possessed a mixed heritage with a mother who the Stern family described as an Irish witch. It occurred to me while listening to their denouncements that I had inherited the looks of the Irish witch with my dark hair, dark eyes, and pale skin. Perhaps my often remarked upon "strangeness" could be traced back to my father's family. I hardly knew my father, but I longed for his return.

Before the war, he had been a small-time actor. According to the Stern family, this was the reason my mother found him intriguing. Even before he married and had a family, he had to supplement his earnings with odd jobs doing stage carpentry or home decorating. He claimed he was not cut out for anything but a life "on the boards." So to earn extra money, he preferred to try his hand at variety, doing conjuring tricks, being the fall guy for established stand-up comedians and even the circus. Just prior to the war, he had several nonspeaking roles in films including the hawk bearer in the Charles Laughton version of *The Life of Henry the Eighth*. His Semitic looks suited him for roles with a biblical setting. He was admirably prepared for the army's Entertainment Corps into which he was drafted.

However, he emerged from that post ill-equipped to support a wife and growing family. His skills as a performer were unfashionable in the late 1940s, and he was temperamentally at odds with the idea of a nine-to-five job following someone else's instructions.

Whenever he found a job, he would end up telling the boss where to go and what he could do with his job. As a result, he was given his cards and arrived home, jobless, in the middle of the day. He did his best to make up for it by taking on private carpentry jobs to fill the gaps between his increasingly infrequent stage appearances. But even this was all to end.

At first, it was good to have him around in his rough khaki uniform, which he continued to wear for a while after he was demobilised from the army. He smelled of snuff and tobacco and shared all kinds of tales about his travels. I loved those times. Michaela was utterly disinterested, but Miranda would sit on his knee and I sat at his feet. We listened to his stories of performances in Burma that were interrupted by American bombing raids. We heard tales of dead Japanese in the jungle and heroic escapes from untold danger.

He brought me a parasol made of waxy paper that he had purchased in Rangoon, an ornamental elephant with ivory tusks that kept falling out, and a strange bank note stained with a red fluid. He explained that he had taken it from the body of a slaughtered Japanese soldier. He also mentioned not to tell anyone because he should not have done that. Even at nine years old, I did not believe this story. I went along with it because I sensed it was important to him that I should see him as a hero whose one thought on encountering a dead enemy soldier was to bring home a souvenir for his little girl. My father's connection with reality was always a bit on the shaky side, a characteristic that made him a great raconteur but a lousy provider.

The rows between my parents were accompanied by my growing awareness that the return of my father from the war was not the beginning of true happiness for the family. My father did not have a proper job and there was not enough money coming in to keep us afloat. It was clear to me that money, or the lack of it, was a major issue between my parents. It was equally clear their issues had little to do with the war. To me, it seemed to have more to do with the fact that they kept on having children. I was wise enough to keep this observation to myself.

My father's response to my mother's demand that he find steady employment was to form a concert party, hardly the answer she had been looking for. Before the introduction of television, concert parties were an extremely popular form of entertainment in the English provinces. My father came in at the tale end of their heyday when he set up "Ross and Dale" (all the way from the Valley of Rossendale) "your very own local concert party."

My father was Ross (actually a name from a branch of his mother's Irish family), and his partner was Chris Dale (actually Tricket). They performed as a comic duo—the backbone of any concert party. He recruited a soprano named Marilyn when my mother (whose voice was far superior) flatly refused to have anything to do with the concert parties. The other members of the group included a baritone who sang solos and duets with Marilyn, a pianist, a conjurer, a ventriloquist, and an illusionist.

For a few years, they toured the working men's clubs of Northeast Lancashire on Friday and Saturday nights with the occasional mid-week matinee bookings. It was not exactly a money-spinner, but it paid the bills and my father was happy. He loved to tell us stories about his "gigs" and the people he met.

What I loved was his makeup box and trunk of costumes and props. When I look back on those days, the image I have of my father is of a man who talked a lot, was full of stories, and lowered his voice when telling them whenever my mother came near. He also rose late in the day with black eyeliner still around his lovely eyes—his best feature.

The local Watch Committees were the bane of the lives of all concert parties.

Their duty was to keep a watch on local morals and to ensure that any form of public entertainment stayed within the bounds of what was then regarded as decency—no swearing, no blasphemy, no undressing, and no sexual innuendos.

My father loved to tell the story of his great aunt on his mother's side, the music hall star, Marie Lloyd.

She was always in trouble with the keeper of public morality, he would tell us, by singing songs that were construed as rude. She was brought up on charges for a song that included a line about a young lady gardener who "sat among the lettuces and peas." She agreed to change it to "she sat among the lettuces and leeks."

He would then laugh like mad and so would I, more to please him than because I entirely got the joke.

One Sunday evening when my father was out on a booking, the local police came to the door of our house.

"Are you Mrs. Rosen?" one officer asked.

"I am," my mother replied thinking my father must have been injured if not killed.

"You *are* the wife of Mr. Eli Rosen, also known as Ross?

"Whatever has he done?" my mother asked in a panic.

"He has caused excessive laughter."

To which my mother responded, "I don't believe it."

As far as she knew, causing laughter was no class of crime. And, the possibility that Ross and Dale had caused laughter of any degree, let alone excessive was, in her experience, a first. "What do you want me to do?" she asked.

"Well, nothing," the policeman replied and then added that there may be a question of bail.

"But I haven't any money," my mother protested, "and I don't know anyone who has. My family all live in London and I don't suppose that they would be too happy about him being arrested, so I'd rather they didn't know."

It appeared that for once in their lives, Ross and Dale had performed to a friendly audience inclined to laugh at anything. Naturally, their laughter was music to the ears of my father and his fall guy. This had a remarkable effect on their performance.

My father used to say that the worst moment in the theatre is when a joke dies and the poor comedian has to continue with his act in front of a silent audience. It had happened to him too often. But on the night in question, he was having a great time ad-libbing and improving on his jokes to the last degree.

The flavour and quality of the jokes were along the lines of, "A Chinaman goes to the dentist and says "toofhurty."

"So what are you doing here at twelve o'clock?" the receptionist replies.

This Sunday crowd found Ross and Dale hilarious, and the men were lapping it up. Unfortunately for them, a member of the local Watch Committee was in the audience as part of their spot check system. One of the rules for permitting the newly introduced Sunday performances was that nothing unseemly was to take place. Unfortunately for Ross and Dale, excessive laughter was deemed unseemly for a Sunday evening. When my father came off stage for a quick change, he was arrested by the local police and taken into custody.

What occurred next brought an end to Ross and Dale's Sunday appearances. Dale was left on stage to fill in with a few conjuring tricks that were to go intentionally wrong while my father changed. After a few minutes, Dale cued my father to come on, Of course, nothing happened.

So Dale repeated, "Well here comes someone who looks like my friend Ross in disguise. He thinks he can fool me, but I've got a surprise for him and I want you to help me." He repeated this several times, and, of course, my father never appeared.

The laughter reached hysterical proportions until finally, a policeman walked on stage to wild shrieks of delight from the audience.

It was some minutes before the audience realized he was the real thing. Dale managed to get the stage manager to bring down the curtain to stop what the policeman announced to be "unseemly goings on."

The trouble was that concert parties did not earn much money for their members. Yet, my father lived as if he were Lawrence Olivier. It wasn't that he spent a lot. It was the lifestyle he adopted. After an evening show, he liked to sleep late, emerging hungry with circles of black makeup around his eyes.

My mother's constant nagging for my father to get a proper job marked the beginning of a fifteen-year war. From time to time, Eli was worn down by the nagging. He'd get up on a Monday morning at seven thirty and go down to the Labour Exchange to get a job, usually as a chippy, or carpenter, on a building site. These episodes usually ended in a row with the boss about how things should be done. Eli refused to compromise and returned home with his pride intact but no money. Only one thing attracted my father to full-time regular work outside the theatre—the feeling of money in his pocket when he was paid. He could stop at the shops on his way home and buy gifts for everyone. He loved coming through the back door shouting, "Father's home." We would all rush to give him a hug. Then he would joyfully parcel out the presents while Miriam stood by. Her eyes flashed disapproval, but she did not want to say anything that would spoil our fun. I realized later that Eli's extravagance was irresponsible—especially in light of his wife's fourth pregnancy, a postwar gift that did not delight her.

There were days when I came home from school to find my father pretending to be engrossed in a book and my mother tight-lipped, not speaking to him. These days were followed by some of the worst evenings of my childhood. Suddenly, unable to contain her anger any longer, my mother would scream at Eli that she wished he was still abroad in the army—although God forbid she wanted the war to go on any longer with what was happening to the Jews. At least when Eli was in the army, the family had a regular income and she knew where the next meal was coming from. She didn't have to deal with all this aggravation, more mouths to feed, and a lazy husband who didn't seem to live in the real world.

Eli would bang the wall with his fist or his head and tell her she knew what his work was when she married him. On more than one occasion, he caused the plaster in the wall to crack. This was followed by days of crumbling bits of plaster on the floor and more nagging from my mother about the length of time it took him to attend to repairs in the house while "Mr. Big Hearted" did jobs for the neighbours for nothing. Everyone loved him and didn't realize what a failure he was. These scenes ended only when Eli walked out into the night regardless of the weather. Those nights, I couldn't sleep until I heard him come back in. Somewhere, at the back of my mind, I was afraid he wouldn't come home. I had no premonition that some years, and yet another child, later it would be my mother who finally walked out never to return.

Chapter Twelve

There was a period when Eli found a job as a stage carpenter at a theatre in Burnley. Understandably enough, he found it difficult not to be a part of the performances. He found an outlet for his theatrical longings by performing in charity shows with some of his former concert party colleagues. Part of this effort produced an annual pantomime that he toured around the various church halls in the Rossendale Valley. For these performances, he enlisted the help of the entire family. Even my mother agreed to make some of the costumes, in particular those of her children. I quite enjoyed the rehearsals, the camaraderie among the cast, even the actual performances. But like my father, I suffered from stage fright.

If I had nerves, my sister Michaela had nightmares. She hated the whole thing and not just the performance bit. She had never been a fan of the theatre, and the word pantomime brought on waves of nausea. She was a most reluctant partner in my father's endeavours and played every trick she could think of to get out of them. She finally decided that her best weapon was incompetence. She never seemed to be bothered about people thinking her stupid whereas the thought horrified me.

Michaela made quite a practice of appearing incapable in order to get out of things she didn't want to do. One year, my father decided that he would depart from the traditional pantomimes, such as *Cinderella* and *Puss in Boots,* and do one based on the popular song, *Rudolf the Red-Nosed Reindeer*.

The night he gathered all the players together to do the casting, I had an uneasy feeling of what was to come. Sure enough, he announced, "Rudolf will be played by my daughters Sophia and Michaela, Sophia will be the front half and Michaela the rear."

Michaela's grip on my hand tightened. "That's it," she muttered under the laughter that accompanied Eli's announcement. "I'm not doing it."

She seemed to be somewhat mortified when she saw the costume our parents designed for the part. It was made out of brown furry material complete with a separate head topped by papier-mâché antlers. The nose was also made of papier-mâché and contained a bulb that would flash to make the nose glow red at appropriate moments. Rudolf's eyes were made of glass. Behind each eye, there was a rubber container with water. This enabled Rudolf to cry whenever the plot called for him to be sad. Michaela was less enchanted when she realized that all these clever bits of lighting the nose, squeezing the rubber tear ducts, and reaching out with a hand disguised as a tongue to take a carrot were to be performed by me. Michaela's role was simply to be bent over with her arms round my waist and her legs in the back legs of the costume.

My father was a complete dictator when it came to his shows. Several intrepid members of the cast pointed out to him, for instance, that reindeers were not known to be partial to carrots. Eli insisted that he knew for a fact that they lived on them. When my mother pointed out that Michaela would get very tired as the back half of Rudolf and that we would both die of the heat if we were on stage too long, he did promise brief appearances during performances. However, he made us wear the costume endlessly during rehearsals. During one of these interminable sessions, Michaela piped up: "It's boring and hot in here. Can I at least have a tail to wag?"

"Absolutely not for the simple reason that reindeers do not have tails," our father replied.

"So who says they cry and have noses that light up?" a fearless cast member ventured to the stifled giggles of the rest of the cast.

Eli drew a deep breath and said, "Let's just get on shall we?"

The rehearsals were terrible. Michaela could see nothing inside the costume and could hear very little. She farted frequently, which reindeers no doubt do but not when someone else is their front half. Fidgety and achy, she kept calling out to our father that she wanted to "take five." Furious with the interruptions, he was calmed down by the rest of the cast, who pointed out that we were only children and it was hot inside the costume.

Eventually, we got our part more or less as he wanted it. Michaela was told to follow my movements and I, who cared much more than she did about the success of the show, faithfully followed Eli's instructions for lighting up the nose, crying, and eating a carrot when given the cue.

The actual performances were something else. When Michaela got fed up, she would suddenly straighten up causing a good deal of turbulence in the middle of Rudolf's body. When my father heard the laughter from the audience, he extemporized, furious though he was. "It must be something he ate," he would say.

My sister saved her revenge for the last night's performance when, by tradition, the cast plays tricks on the orchestra and the stage hands on the cast. Eli held up a carrot to Rudolf and said, "Come on boy. Don't be upset. Have a lovely carrot." On cue, as I was prepared to stick out Rudolf's tongue to take it, Michaela started to walk backwards. I had no choice but to follow. My father pursued us with the carrot and continued with the scripted dialogue, "Oh, you like carrots I see. Well, here's another for a good boy."

Michaela succeeded in backing Rudolf into the wings. My father was forced to say, "He seems to have gone off carrots," and missed out on a chunk of the action.

The audience and the rest of the cast loved it, Eli did not. At the first opportunity, he yelled at both of us. "I hope that was meant to be a joke. Well, it went too far."

Michaela, who knew exactly what she was doing, piped up, "It was my fault. I made Sophia go backwards."

"For that," stormed Eli, "you will never be in another pantomime, not while I'm in charge."

Michaela pretended to cry, the little minx. I admired my sister then, and I still do. I knew she would sail through life, avoiding anything she didn't want to do and getting away with it.

Another memory of my father's exploits in the world of entertainment is much sadder. He was dedicated to raising a laugh or at least some kind of response from his audience. It was torture for him to face a silent crowd. He preferred an empty theatre to stony silence.

"They were afraid to crack their faces," he would say if he came home after such an experience.

At the opening of every show, he would bound onto the stage and announce, "Hi there. I want to hear you say, "Hi-yah Ross.""

He would then tell the audience their response was not loud enough, so he would try again. "Let's hear you. I couldn't hear that. So, once again, altogether now, "Hiyah Ross!""

He would repeat this until the rafters rang. Once when the audience wasn't responding to suit him, he took a handful of coins from his pocket and threw them at the audience. "Whatever it cost you to come here take your money back and go home with your misery," he shouted at them. "Ring down the curtain, that's it for tonight."

Of course, my mother was upset. "You're supposed to earn money not throw it away," she admonished. "You'll never get another gig."

He did though. Maybe because people wanted to see what he would do next. My father never lost his sense of pride nor his ability to turn adversity into a good story. He was a born raconteur. He amused his children and friends with his tales of his attempts at regular work and the dramas that ensued during his life of "treading the boards," both past and present.

For my mother, it was a lifetime of disappointment, unfulfilled expectations, and poverty—not at all what she had expected when she married her handsome actor. She was not equipped for it. As time went by, she became more and more concerned with her day-by-day survival and less and less with the development of her daughters and little Sean, her only son and her fourth child.

Chapter Thirteen

When I was going on eleven, my father had been home from the war for about two years and the war between my parents had been waging for about the same time. It bothered me a lot. I used to lie awake at night listening to their arguments and wondering what I could do to make them be friends. I tried to figure out what could have gone wrong to make people who had apparently, and against considerable opposition, married for love, become so angry with one another all the time.

The main issue seemed to centre on money. So why didn't my father get a proper job like other fathers? The phrase "too many mouths to feed" came up a lot in their rows. So why did they keep having children? They even argued about cigarettes—who had smoked whose and where the other had hidden them. So why didn't they stop smoking?

This question gave me an idea. I had seen an advertisement for decoy cigarettes. When smoked, these made the smoker sick and resolve never to want to smoke again. I diligently saved up the money I was paid for doing an elderly neighbour's errands and sent away for a packet of the decoy cigarettes. My scheme was to present these to my parents on their wedding anniversary.

The cigarettes arrived in a padded envelope addressed to me. Naturally, my mother wanted to know what was in it. I said it was a surprise for her. I was so excited and could hardly wait for their anniversary to arrive. When it did, I presented the cigarettes wrapped, in the absence of any fancy paper, in toilet roll. I formally announced to them, "I hope my gift will lead to years of happy marriage."

Their delight at seeing what appeared to be a regular packet of cigarettes soon vanished when they read the accompanying leaflet. My mother's bafflement turned to anger when she said, "Sophia, do not try to run our lives."

My father gave me a hug and said, "Thanks for the thought darling. But you see, we don't want to give up smoking. I am afraid you have wasted your pocket money." I was bitterly disappointed, and my hopes of saving their marriage were shattered. I had to admit that it was not within my power. At that point, I decided I would leave home as soon as possible and never get married.

Once again, it was school that showed me the way. A month after the wedding anniversary episode, I was scheduled to start attending the local grammar or senior school. I had gained admittance after my eleven-plus exam earlier in the year. I had been nervous about sitting the exam. However, I found it to be ridiculously easy. I even convinced myself that I had been given a paper intended for students wishing to go to the secondary modern school—a mistake that would not be discovered until it was too late and I found myself attending the wrong school. Looking around the examination room and seeing people struggle to complete their papers long after I had put my pen down, I was convinced something was wrong. I worried about this every night until the results announced that I had passed and had gained entrance to the grammar school. I was overjoyed. My parents were not.

Their reservations were based on the necessity to provide me with a uniform. The result of this particular quarrel was a note written to Grandmother Stern enclosing the list of clothes, equipment, and books I would need. I wrote separately to tell her the good news that I had passed. By return letter, I received congratulations from my grandmother and Rosa that they had never had any doubt I would pass. They also sent postal orders to cover the cost of outfitting me for the start of school. Every year of my school life thereafter, my Stern relations clothed and equipped me so that my schooling would not be a burden on my parents. By the time I reached the sixth form, I received a grant from the local authority for books. And, joy of joys, my scholarships to university enabled me not only to cover my own expenses but to be able to give money to my parents and buy presents for my siblings.

My father eventually rejoiced in my academic achievements. My mother never understood why I needed them or so it seemed to me. I wanted my parents to be proud of me, but I concluded that only Rosa and Grandmother Stern really were. I recall my mother telling her friend Florrie Manson that she had sacrificed a lot for my higher education. This made me feel guilty that I had not gone out to work as soon as I reached the age where I could leave school.

Guilty or not, there is no doubt in my mind that school empowered me though it was not, of course, without its quota of anxieties. Belonging to a family with no money was reason enough to feel defensive. Being half-Jewish and half-Irish made me not only a unique phenomenon but also the object of adjectives ranging from "weird" to "stuck-up." Being poor meant not being able to go on school journeys, being half-Jewish meant that my schoolmates thought we probably had the money but were too mean to spend it, and being half-Irish meant I should have been stupid. But I was not. This produced the "weird" word that I declined to pretend I was, which in turn, made me "stuck-up." More often, I was called the swot. Because if you were top of the class, that's what you had to be, a person who did nothing but study.

My secondary school years could have been miserable. In fact, on the whole, they were not. But I must say, in some ways, going to grammar school at eleven marked the end of my childhood and the beginning of more adult anxieties and preoccupations.

For instance, there was a time, perhaps as long as a year, when I was convinced I was turning into a boy. I was very small and skinny in my childhood. This fear was something that I wouldn't have told Rosa even if she had been available. For one thing, I was worried that my fears would be confirmed. But on the other hand, I did not want to be laughed at.

I think this particular anxiety was fired by a girl called Vera. Although we were roughly the same age, she was twice my size. She told me I had the body of a boy. Looking around me in the girls' changing rooms at school, I could see she had a point. All the other girls who were eleven and twelve seemed to have breasts; I was still as flat as a pancake. Furthermore, girls in my class had their periods and brought notes to school to excuse them from swimming lessons because they had to wear what were quite disgustingly known as "jam rags." I inspected myself daily for the signs, but knew that such a fate had not befallen me. I was convinced it was never going to.

I certainly hadn't been well versed in sex education. Even by the age of eleven and twelve, I had only the vaguest idea of what boys looked liked when they were undressed. When my little brother Sean was born, I inquired of my mother why it was that he had two tails. By the time he was two, and I had learned that one of the tails was known as a penis, I had observed that given a little massage this appendage would spring to life and change its shape. I could see no such development in my own nether regions despite daily inspections.

But my fears would not be quashed. Indeed, they were exacerbated in my first year at school by my adoration of a young, female Latin teacher. I was thrilled to discover her first name (Ruth) and I scoured the poetry books for references to it. It was then that I discovered there was a whole book devoted to Ruth in the Bible. So I copied out bits that I thought applied to her and left them on her desk. I never discovered whether she realized that I had a "crush" on her as it was called. Perhaps teachers of adolescents are accustomed to it.

At any rate, she very sensibly avoided anything which could be construed as encouragement and, in time, I recovered from my crush without experiencing humiliation. At the time, however, it was further proof that I was really a boy since what girl falls in love with a female teacher? Of course, I knew nothing about lesbianism or how natural schoolgirl crushes are. I was saved the worry of wondering whether I was gay while suffering in ignorance of the regular rituals of adolescence.

Girls would confide in their best friends, who naturally passed on the confidences to other best friends, when they started their periods and when they were subsequently indisposed. Apart from confiding about this personal topic, the girls in my class would regularly report on how many pubic hairs they had growing. I was ignorant of the fact that boys also had pubic hairs since my brother had none. This was further proof that since I shared his deficiency, I must also really be a boy. Anyone knowing me post adolescence would no doubt give a horse laugh at this self-inflicted torture since I became so utterly feminine as to make my worries unbelievable.

This period of anxiety lasted throughout my first year at school. In fact, I was fourteen before the onset of my menses. But by that time, I had built up a reputation as being a good kisser of boys and was in love with a young man in my class with the unfortunate name of David Pickup. I no longer feared an imminent sex change and my anxieties had moved on.

I fell in love several times during my school years, apart from the young Latin teacher and David Pickup. I was in love with a boy prodigy who was tragically killed during a skiing holiday with his parents. Love befell me again with the handsome, clever brother of one of my friends. He was several years older than me, and I honestly believe he never knew of my existence.

But my true love, which lasted long after I had left school behind, was very different. It was a Rosa kind of love and the object of it was my English teacher. Her name was Ella, and she came from Arundel in Sussex. From the first day she entered our classroom clutching her gown around her thin body, we established a rapport that I came to believe was based on a mutual vulnerability and devotion to English literature.

Naturally, it took time for us to discover each other's sensitivities, and she was no doubt quicker. She was curious about my background, in which no other teacher had taken the least interest. She soon realized that my family had no money. By telling me quietly that she had a spare ticket and not to say a word she saved me the embarrassment of having to say I could not attend a performance of *The Merchant of Venice* at the Library Theatre in Manchester. My nightmare then focused on whether the outing would be in school uniform. She relieved my fear of possessing nothing else decent to wear by announcing, to groans all around, that school uniform was compulsory.

She was not a person you would notice in a crowd, rather like me really, except she was less coloured as it were. She was small and very thin. Indeed, her nickname was "boney." Her features were almost colourless—pale skin and hair. Her eyes behind huge glasses were always red rimmed. She walked very quickly, stooping forward with her gown pulled tightly around her. She spoke correct English but had a rather nasal way of speaking. In other words, not a very pretty picture, but I was crazy about her.

I persuaded my mother that I needed glasses so she took me off to the optician. Unfortunately, he said I had a slight stigmatism but otherwise eyesight as good as any he had recently tested. With that path blocked, I took to smearing my eyes with golden eye ointment so that I would look like my beloved teacher. I clutched my clothes around me as I stooped and hurried across the hall. I even started to talk down my nose. Finally it was she who said to me, "You know Sophia my dear, they say that imitation is the sincerest form of flattery but I don't need it."

I got the point. I loved her even more for not ridiculing me.

She introduced the class to Shakespeare, Marlow, Milton, Donne, and Pope. Later, we studied Ruskin, James, and Hardy with such understanding and commitment that I was not the only one who was utterly devoted to her, but I had more cause than most. When my parents saw how much interest she took in me, they decided she was a possible benefactor. To my mortification, whenever times were particularly hard, they sent me off to "borrow" money from her—twenty pounds here and twenty-five pounds there.

I hated it, but at the same time, I felt a strong responsibility to help my parents. I forced myself to go through with it. She always complied and told me there was no hurry to pay her back. She understood how painful the whole business was for me.

My parents never did return the money, but I did—every penny of it as soon as I received my first State Scholarship money for the university. She was the teacher who persuaded my mother to allow me to take up that scholarship and attend Liverpool University to study English Literature in the department headed by the renowned Shakespeare scholar, Professor Kenneth Muir.

My favourite teacher had her own vulnerability, which was one of the sources of the bond between us. She was the third wife of the chemistry master, commonly known as "Test Tube Charlie." As such, he was subjected to unkind gossip on the lines of his having disposed of the other two wives by "chemical means."

"Watch how she's disappearing before our eyes," the kids would say.

"She's not long for this world," one of the tea ladies told me.

Test Tube Charlie was, in fact, as kind and lovely a man as you would wish to meet. He was a man who must have been very handsome in his younger days. But the rumours persisted. One day, a very bossy, very Lancastrian tea lady, the head of the team, told me, "There are things you ought to know about your friends. Test Tube Charlie has definitely murdered his first two wives by poisoning them. They were both rich so he has inherited all their money. They had no children so your precious English teacher decided to be number three. She knew alright what he'd been up to. Because she's so much younger, she thinks she'll see him out. But judging by the state of her eyes, he's already on the job and she'll be lucky to get away with it."

This story troubled me so much I couldn't sleep. I needed advice. I didn't believe it for a minute, but my dilemma was whether or not to tell my teacher what they were saying. If only Rosa had been around. She was the only one I could have talked to about it.

Finally, I decided I should tell. The result was a huge uproar. The tea lady was sacked, I was sent to Coventry (not to be spoken to) by the other pupils for snitching, and many of the teachers were distinctly cool to me. It all blew over in time, and I learned a valuable lesson—never to repeat gossip or as Ella herself put it to me, "Only pass on the good things that people say about others."

The theatrical productions were one of the highlights of my school days. It was such a relief not to be directed by my father. I was not expected to understand a half-intelligible instruction on first hearing nor give the outstanding performance of the evening. I was simply another amateur child actress.

It's true that my first experience is not one I recall with pleasure. The lower school was putting on an operetta, which involved gypsy costumes and flowers that came to life. I was one of the flowers and hated my costume. As the smallest in the class, I was selected to be a violet. I was cloaked in a deep purple tunic with handkerchief points, purple stockings, and a purple cap with a pointed top complete with a little yellow flower perched on it. It was years before I could look purple in the face again.

My roles grew in status as I progressed through the school. I played Juliet opposite Romeo. As Eliza Doolittle in *Pygmalion*, I was obliged to use the word "Pygmalion" for the word "bloody" in Eliza's famous line "Not bloody likely."

A new English teacher joined the staff at the school and at once set about planning productions of Gilbert and Sullivan on which he was an expert. "G & S," he once hollered out to a largely unenthusiastic class, "are an essential part of your culture as English men and women, which for these purposes, Sophia Rosen, includes you."

"My mother," I informed him, "used to sing with the D'Oyly Carte Opera Company, so we listen to Gilbert and Sullivan all the time at home."

"Do you indeed?" he responded. "Do you think your mother would like to come and sing for us?"

My mother would not. But my audacious revelation was probably the reason why I was cast as one of the four little maids in the *Mikado* and a leading chorister in *Trial By Jury*. When I was about to move into the A-level classes, my headmaster wrote on my end-of-year report, "I hope and believe she has come to the end of a rather frivolous stage. If so, she will be a worthy sixth-form member."

Rosa laughed her head off. My mother considered it grounds for leaving school.

Chapter Fourteen

One thing I have inherited from my mother, and my children from me, is an extreme, perhaps even neurotic, fastidiousness in matters of personal and household cleanliness. Miriam often said, "No one is too poor to buy a bar of soap." So our shabby clothes were made even shabbier with constant washing and ironing.

My mother's fussiness was legendary among our neighbours. My mother was particularly close to one neighbour who also was a "foreigner" who came from Leicester. Perhaps that was the mutual bond. She tried to persuade my mother that it was only necessary to change our knickers once a week. This suggestion horrified all of us and put their friendship at risk.

She was yet another Florrie and the second or third wife of a former sailor—famous for his attachment to the local pub. One of the favourite games of the local kids was to lead this poor man, when he was staggering home in his "cups," to the wrong door.

Florrie's notoriety was based on her reputation as a sex mad woman. She had a string of lovers in her history despite a limp, far from beautiful features, and a penchant for crude language.

She brought to the marriage a multicoloured parrot that, according to the local gossip, had been a farewell gift from another seafaring former lover. The bird's vocabulary was even more colourful than Florrie's. The two carried on a running feud as if he resented having been made a gift to her.

Visitors to the house, which were many, more on account of the parrot's repertoire than Florrie's appalling cooking, were greeted with squawks of, "Bugger off," or once inside, "Shut the door you silly sod." They were also informed, "Florrie's had a fuck." And when Florrie commanded it to shut up or she put a blanket over his cage, it would respond,

"Change your knickers, Florrie." Advice which, by her own admission, she followed only once a week.

I disapproved of my mother's friendship with Florrie. It was quite inexplicable to me and to my father since neither parent, despite their theatrical connections, ever swore or told an off-colour joke. Yet Florrie reduced my mother to a giggling teenager hinting at nights of indescribable passion with my father and a few others in her past. Listening to my mother confiding to her friend that the nightdress she was ironing could tell a few stories made me want to throw up. Not because I believed it, I did not, but because I felt it was unworthy of my mother. What did it mean? Had she missed out in the sex department despite having all these children? Or was she just trying like a child to impress her friend?

But at one time, I suspected my mother was having an illicit relationship with the local dentist. I had already formed the impression that she was more interested in sex than my father. This was based solely on overhearing her tell her evidently half-asleep husband to "get on with it."

My suspicions about the dentist were aroused because Miriam was a notorious coward when it came to anything to do with health, especially her teeth. Suddenly, she was going twice a week to a dentist's surgery without a murmur. Furthermore, she only had a few teeth of her own, in her bottom jaw. She had followed the ludicrous contemporary fashion of removing the entire top row of teeth in order to acquire a gleaming set of false teeth. Every woman who peopled my childhood had artificial teeth.

What could Mr. Longbottom, the local dentist, be doing with all these women except having affairs with them? I confronted my mother by asking why she went to see him so often. She replied, "He is trying to save my few bottom teeth from suffering the same fate as their siblings on the top row."

The fashion for false teeth had now been denounced as dangerous rubbish. My scepticism of this explanation was dispelled only after reading the *Rossendale Free Press*. Apparently, Mr. J. Longbottom, dentist, had committed suicide by inhaling his own anaesthetic gas. It had been disclosed that he had earned a fortune by dabbing oil of cloves on patients' teeth twice a week for years—thanks to the gullibility of dozens of followers of yet another dubious fashion. I never knew what my mother felt on reading this, just as she never knew that I had suspected her of infidelity.

I have often reflected on, what seemed to me at the time, my mother's familiarity with our neighbours. She got along with them remarkably well considering the vast differences in backgrounds. Maybe it was a reflection of her loneliness and possibly also of the already well established alienation from my father. She spent a lot of time gossiping with the women who lived on either side of us as well as with her friend Florrie. Yet when my mother finally left, she did so without saying goodbye to anyone. There was absolutely no contact from that day on with her former neighbours and friends.

So complete was her break with my father and Rossendale that she destroyed photographs from the years she lived there. She refused to entertain any reminiscences or attempts to engage her in any conversation pertaining to those times. Indeed, she developed a pathological fear of running into anyone with Rossendale connections of which my father was the ultimate embodiment. She never uttered his name, wrote him a word, nor inquired after his well-being once she walked out of the Edgeside house. It was worse than if he had died. It was as if he had never existed at all, though she was married to him for twenty-five years and had borne him five children.

Eli, however, frequently asked me how she was and was close to being distressed when he finally heard she had died. It appears that my mother was an expert in denial. She was capable of excluding or ignoring whatever caused her pain or discomfort. It may be some kind of gift—one that I do not possess.

I remember, willingly or otherwise, the pain of witnessing my parents disintegrating relationship and the elements that contributed to it. Undoubtedly, one of those was the lack of money. This affected all of us directly. But I was the one who was always sent out to borrow or *schnorer* as the Sterns called it. Perhaps on account of my manners, my diminutive size, or my way with words, I was considered the best *schnorer* in the family.

I would stand outside a neighbour's door, half hoping they would not be home. But I was acutely aware that my family really did need a loaf of bread or half a packet of tea, and there was no other way of obtaining these items. If the neighbour answered the door, I had to speak out. I never beat about the bush but came straight out with the request I had been sent to make, "I'm sorry to be here again Mrs. Woodstock, but you know Mum would not ask if she didn't have to. If you can lend us some sugar she will return it at the end of the week."

My direct method worked. I never came away emptyhanded, but I hated doing it. I swore that if I ever had children, which seemed unlikely to me at the time, they would never go through this humiliation on my behalf. Even harder to cope with was the accumulated guilt about the number of items that were never returned. This was further compounded by the anger I felt, but could not express to my parents, when I was sent to beg for cigarettes. It seemed that everyone around me smoked. I considered cigarettes as a force of evil whose attraction was a mystery to me. Adults blamed it on the war. "We needed something to soothe our nerves," they would say.

And of course, once the war was history, they were hopeless addicts. There was a culture surrounding cigarettes, involving some kind of class snobbery. Grandmother Stern and Rosa smoked du Maurier. My mother smoked Craven A. Woodbines were at the bottom of the smoker's scale and were my father's preference. It didn't matter to me—they all made me nauseous. My distaste was worsened by my parent's fights over who had smoked the other's last fag or the sight of Eli trying to make a new cigarette out of the stubs of old ones or tea leaves.

When I was sent to "borrow" five cigarettes, I became a rebel, an angry antismoking campaigner. I pretended the neighbours were out or had no cigarettes to spare. But it did no one any good. My parents just became more irritable and quarrelsome to the point where I would volunteer to ask someone else. Miraculously, I would find the original targets had returned home with cigarettes to spare.

I found borrowing cigarettes as shameful as asking for money. My mother had an unerring sense about who had money to spare and who had more than they admitted. This awareness was probably borne of being raised among people who always had enough and the current desperation of having nothing with as many as seven hungry mouths to feed.

A proud woman, Mother could never bring herself to do the begging. Therefore, she sent me, her eldest, capable child with a strong instinct for survival. "Neither a borrower nor a lender be," Grandmother Stern used to say. This advice was steadfastly ignored by her daughter. Mother borrowed from necessity and would willingly have loaned to anyone had she had anything worth borrowing.

In common with almost all the neighbours, we shopped at the local grocery store buying everything on "tick." The shopkeeper recorded our purchases expecting to be paid at the end of the week when, presumably, the wages would come in. Except in our case, this frequently didn't occur. The system was a boon to both customer and grocer, the former buying more than he could actually afford and the latter charging top prices. Since everyone was doing it, I had no scruples about asking the grocer to add whatever I had been sent to buy on the book.

But going to the coalman's yard to ask for a hundred weight of coal on "tick" was another matter. It was a long walk through unlit streets to the coal yard. Upon my arrival, I was greeted by a big, black, smelly dog. After terrifying me almost to death, it proceeded to dribble all over me in apparent friendship. This coal man was unlike "Poor John," the one who was besotted with my Aunt Alicia. This coal man was the one potential benefactor of the Rosen family who was impervious to my appeals. He turned me away on more than one occasion with a sharp,

"Not on your life young woman. Be off with you."

I hated being poor. I was angry with my parents for having so many children, for their constant bickering, and for wanting to conform to the ways of the local community. Most of this I kept to myself. In part, I realized that I was being unfair, but occasionally, I rebelled. Once when my mother was busy bathing the new baby, Sean, she asked me to go next door to borrow some milk. I was doing my homework and resented the baby, the interruption, and the need once more to go on the borrow. I burst out,

"No I won't. And I hate you."

It was an unspeakably awful thing to say to my poor, unhappy, overworked mother, and I knew it. I grabbed my school bag and ran out of the house up to the hills above the estate where I often went to think in peace and quiet. After a couple of hours, feeling hungry and knowing that running away from home with no money was not a realistic option, I walked slowly home. I lifted the back door latch as silently as I could and hesitatingly entered the kitchen where both my parents were standing. Before I could open my mouth to speak the carefully rehearsed words of apology I intended to offer my mother, Eli did something he had never done before and never did again. He hit me hard on the left side of my face making my head sing with pain, "Don't you ever dare speak to your mother like that again," he said.

I did not cry even though I wanted to. "You say worse things to her," I replied.

Then fearing another assault, I ran up to my room. I took a box of paints out of my cupboard, licked my finger, and rubbed it in the crimson palette. Using the dressing table mirror, I carefully drew a line from my ear down my left cheek. When I was satisfied that it looked realistic, I let out a great scream that brought my mother running up the stairs.

"My ear hurts, my ear hurts," I wailed. Miriam took one look at my face and was fooled.

"I think he has perforated my ear drum," I added.

I quickly wished I hadn't for Miriam went into a panic.

"We have to get you to the doctor; do you think you can walk?"

In our circumstances, getting to the doctor was no easy task. We had no car and no telephone to call a taxi. Finally, I persuaded her to let me "wash away the blood" with warm water, put cotton wool in my ear, take an aspirin, and see how I was in the morning. Miriam was easily persuaded; Eli, who flinched under her chastisement, less so. But the technical difficulties of getting me to a hospital or even to the local doctor eventually overcame his fear. No more was heard about my bad behaviour and my naughtiness was rewarded with a bit of pampering. Years later, I confessed what I had done to my elderly father. He didn't remember it.

I used to enjoy getting my father to talk about the past, especially about his early days in the theatre and about his parents. His father, known as Matt the Jew, was apparently something of a Dublin legend. While Eli was an excellent raconteur, when it came to understanding the fears and aspirations of an adolescent girl, he was hopeless. If I told him I was worried about a forthcoming exam, he might say something such as, "What you need is a cigarette." When he heard I was going up to the university, or I complained I had been a wallflower at a school dance, he would warn me, "Keep men at arms length." Whatever anguish he may have suffered, he kept to himself. Perhaps that effort left him no energy to spare for his daughter's problems.

My reservations about seeking my mother's support continued throughout my life—possibly to my own detriment. The result was I grew and matured without the benefit of parental guidance though I knew I was loved. I continued to miss Rosa, whose sympathy and understanding I really needed. But even with her, I felt the need to edit my thoughts and feelings to protect her from worrying about me. And oddly, I felt an enormous responsibility to my parents as if it were up to me to ease their burdens.

I can honestly say I never felt any resentment about this. Things were as they were. I accepted my role as I accepted the colour of my eyes. Later on, I was able to rationalise the deprivations of my childhood and be grateful for the self-dependency they instilled in me. I ended up with more than my parents ever had, and they must be at least partially responsible for whatever natural resources I can claim.

It may be fashionable to blame an emotionally deprived childhood for whatever failures or weaknesses have pursued one into adulthood, but I have never been able to do this. Neither have my siblings. We have all turned out alright, relatively sane, relatively comfortable and happy. The one area where, perhaps, a psychiatrist could say I am deficient is in my feelings about the death of my mother. The truth is that I do not miss her. I miss Rosa like mad but not my mother.

Chapter Fifteen

My mother was a great reader; Dickens was her absolute favourite author. My father was this wonderful storyteller. But they lacked interpersonal communication skills. I never knew them to sit down and have a good talk with their children or with each other. No one could blame television, as we didn't have one. Over the years, the incompatibility of my parents deepened. They found less and less pleasure in one another's company.

After one of their frequent rows, my father would take himself off, slamming the door behind him to go for a walk in the lower hills around the estate. If he had followed in the Irish tradition, he would have returned the worse for drink. But he lacked the money, even if he'd had the inclination. So he used up his anger and frustration in planning one of his shows.

In this respect, I followed in his footsteps. Never willing to cry or complain when I was upset, I would retreat to my favourite place, the spot called Jack Lodge. It was a small lake situated between two banks of hills. This was a place my mother preferred us not to frequent because it was so isolated. But in defiance of her wishes, and without her knowledge, I would make myself a sandwich, take a bottle of Vimto (a local nonalcoholic brew dark in colour and rather medicinal in taste), stuff them in an oilskin shopping bag with my homework, and wander off.

I climbed the hill, or brew as we called it, to the next highest level of the estate. Then I walked along a road known simply as "The Top Road" and climbed another hill passing through farm yards until I arrived at the lodge. Young boys, including my brother Sean, used to venture up there in the summer holidays to catch tiddlers. My brother is the only person I have ever known who could catch them in his mouth. But other than the boys, the place was very little visited.

My mother's anxiety about Jack Lodge was due to its notoriety as a lovers' haunt. Supposedly, a young local girl was
raped here. Subsequently, according to the tale, the young
girl gave birth to a mentally retarded child. But I loved Jack
Lodge, especially on the rare days when the sun shone and
there was no breeze.

When I had finished my homework, I would allocate myself other tasks, such as reading a prescribed section of the
following year's set text. Only then would I allow myself to
read Daphne du Maurier (not related to the cigarettes by the
same name as I was relieved to learn) or Georgette Heyer.
All my schoolgirl books except my favourite Angela Brazils
had been passed on to Michaela as I considered I had grown
out of them.

At exam times, I would make myself a strict study sched-
ule—much of which was also done up at Jack Lodge. The
damp ground and the prickly grass that cut my fingers were
not ideal conditions for studying. However, it clearly beat
the noisy Rosen household where no one had a room to himself, and I was liable to be called upon to help out with the
household chores. I was unusually firm about taking time
out to do my studies and refused to feel guilty about it.

All kinds of tricks were employed, especially by my siblings, to induce that guilt. They would be astonished if they
knew that my single-minded devotion to my studies has not
protected me from recurrent nightmares in which I am insuf-
ficiently prepared for an exam.

Theatricals provided the means for another escape route
from my home. I presume my interest was stimulated by my
parents' background. However, if there had been something
genetic about it, my sisters and my brother did not inherit the
gene.

Despite my parents' vocations, neither my father nor my
mother ever attended one of my school performances. They
pleaded a lack of the right thing to wear.

I sympathized with their pride, but I was hurt.

Things between my parents irretrievably worsened during my school days. My mother's middle-class expectations, damaged though they had been during her long exile from all she knew, nevertheless persisted. Eli's income could not possibly match her needs. He tried but was simply not cut out to hold down a regular job. He found timekeeping anything from irksome to unreasonable, and he never developed a willingness to take orders. He always found a reason for telling the foreman of whatever building or carpentry job he was currently engaged on "to go to hell." He would come home in the middle of the day with half a pay packet, if he was lucky, and the rows would start again.

He undertook private work on the weekends. While he completed the work to the customer's satisfaction, he could never bring himself to ask for the money. That turned out to be my job. My mother would instruct me to present the bill and wait on the customer's doorstep until I received the payment. Money, or the lack of it, continued to be a major issue. After fights about not having any money, never going anywhere, children needing new shoes, etc., my parents embarked on their long silences. At these times, they either communicated via the nearest child or with written notes.

"Tell your father his dinner is in the oven," Miriam would write.

Eli would reply with a note left on the table, "The stew needed more salt."

They could go on like this for months to the point where it became normal. Then suddenly, with no explanations, there would be a rapprochement. Then once again the talking followed by the fighting would begin.

One such reconciliation resulted in Miriam's fifth pregnancy and the birth of my baby sister Esther. This was an episode of traumatic proportions for me. I found the situation excruciatingly embarrassing. I knew of no other parents who were still "at it" at their age, let alone producing offspring. I told no one about my mother's condition until Esther's birth was a *fait accompli* and could no longer be denied. She was born at home in January 1953 with a midwife in attendance. This was just a few months after my Grandmother Stern had died.

It was a difficult birth that left Miriam unable to run the house properly for weeks. The burden of domestic chores that fell on me dramatically increased. I was also responsible for the frequent errands to purchase nappies and other essentials on "tick." I not only provided meals for the family but, with the help of a neighbour's washing machine, ensured that clean clothes were available for everyone.

In the year of Esther's birth, I was taking my O level exams and studying for A levels in the lower sixth form. The Minister of Education had issued a retrogressive decree that students, who were not sixteen by September first, could not take their O level exams. As my birthday fell nine days past that date, I had to enter the sixth form and start preparing for A levels and university entrance while still maintaining a grasp of all my O level subjects.

In conjunction with my additional household chores, this was too much for me. I suffered a breakdown with repeated bouts of nausea and vomiting. I did not want to leave my bed in the morning. My paranoia about someone creeping up the stairs at night to molest me increased. I became more and more obsessive and composed lists of things in my head that I had to do. I went over them time and time again, deciding how I was going to deal with it all. At the end of this process, I convinced myself that I had forgotten something and would start the whole business over again. I uncharacteristically burst into tears for no good reason. Hives appeared all over the trunk of my body. I told myself I was stunted in my growth, had stupid hair, and was terminally unattractive. If that wasn't enough, I felt pressured that I came from a family that had no money and was always at war. There was no joy to be had from life.

Even my excellent exam results, when they finally came, did nothing to cheer me up. In the end, my English teacher came to see my mother to suggest that I needed to see a doctor. My parents were unsure about this as they had apparently noted nothing serious, but finally, my mother and Michaela took me to see the general practitioner. After my examination, I was pronounced anaemic and exhausted. The recommended elixir was a long summer holiday. I immediately spoke up and said my mother needed me at home and we could not afford a holiday. Miriam's pride could not let this stand. As much as she needed me, she volunteered to ask Rosa if I could stay with her for the summer holidays.

A delighted note of acceptance with a postal order for the coach fare arrived by return mail. I resumed my annual trip to London, though from that year forward, it was only to be with Rosa, since my beloved grandmother had passed away.

The reassurance of Rosa's belief in my abilities and the exciting future they would lead me to worked wonders. After five weeks, I was able to return to the chaotic Rosen household and my studies with something approaching pleasure.

I loved these journeys on the Yelloway coaches, which prior to motorways took an entire day to travel from Rossendale to London with several rest stops. As reading made me nauseous, I spent the time thinking, observing, and imagining. I imagined what life must be like for the people who lived in the semidetached homes that lined the suburban roads of the towns and cities we passed through. Were they ordered, without crisis, comfortable, and calm? Were they nothing like the home I had left and would be returning to? My initial thoughts envied lives that carried no great responsibility or challenge—men tended the gardens, women joined local clubs, and the children all had a room of their own.

I knew I could have a life like that if I wanted it. At one point, I told myself that a life such as that with which I had invested the occupiers of suburbia would be dull after a week or two, not at all of the kind to which I aspired. I knew my horizons would be wider—just how wide I could not have imagined. I was of an age where I felt there was nothing I wanted to be that I could not achieve. After five weeks of Rosa's love and patience, this was truly how I felt.

My mental accounting on the return journey to Rossendale was done in a positive mood. I felt there was little I could not tackle. I knew I would never be an opera singer to fulfil my mother's thwarted ambition, nor a poet. I recognized myself as a fairly prosaic person. But I could be an ice-skater or a linguist or a top lawyer or a film director. It was in this mood that I returned to my exhausted parents.

The period that followed was a time of intensive study and academic achievement. It also marked the blossoming of my social conscience and campaigning spirit. While girls around me were falling in love and/or planning to marry a rich man, I decided I would never marry at all, being less than enchanted by my daily observance of what being married meant. As for riches, I not only had no intention of marrying into them, I wasn't at all interested in accumulating them. I strongly disapproved of privilege and wealth. As far as I was concerned, all income had to be earned and the people who earned it should have control of the means of production. In other words, I was a right little communist in the making.

At this stage, I was unaware of how difficult I was to get along with. What I did notice was that friends who seemed to have enjoyed my company earlier in our school years were less keen to pursue our friendship as we grew older. For instance, they were disinclined to engage in debates with me about the incompatibility of the twin ideals of equality and freedom or whether there could ever be something called absolute truth. If they did join me in one heated discussion on these lines, they shied away from a second round.

The headmaster wrote at the bottom of my final school report, "If Sophia can strike a balance between intensity and frivolity she will thrive at university. Her undoubted talents have yet to find a direction."

I was incensed. Whatever direction my talents eventually took it would not be toward affection for my former headmaster. That was one promise that I have kept. The frivolity bit really hurt. Didn't the man realize that a girl without money, without social position, of uncertain identity, and basically a foreign implant had to deflect sympathy by turning everything into a joke? I observed people who shared some of my social disadvantages but who were not as able to turn sympathy into a grudging admiration. A girl whose parents didn't attend school functions and never participated in school journeys had to nip the teasing and the gibes in the bud by never allowing anyone to feel sorry for her. Long before I left school, I had observed that achievers with a sharp tongue, who seemed happy to be what they were, did not attract pity and were rendered less vulnerable.

While I was still in school, I founded a branch of the Council for Education in World Citizenship, commonly known as CEWC. I organized meetings after school for discussions on what it meant to be a world citizen and lectures by eminent local people who could be said to embrace the principles of CEWC.

These rules were vague enough to be open to various and, not infrequently, contradictory interpretations. But as far as I was concerned, a person interested in being educated in world citizenship had to believe that nationalism was the root of all evil. I extended my theory to include the family unit as the source of the tribalism and exclusivity that I saw blighting the fabric of society. I was full of clichés as I set out on a course that seemed designed to alienate everyone around me—starting with my parents. Only Rosa found it in her to applaud my efforts to forge a philosophy of my own, while gently begging to differ with many of my views.

These opinions were considerably tempered during my final months at school when I fell head over heals in love with the local Labour MP (Member of Parliament). Thus it was that Tony Greenwood, the handsome debonair MP for Rossendale, saved me from going to university as an insufferable dogmatist with invisible emotions. He also caused me to transfer my adolescent affections from female teachers to equally unattainable forty-something politicians. Tony Greenwood had a daughter barely younger than me. However, that did not deter me from believing that one day he would wake up in the morning to the realization that he was in love with me.

I became a Tony Greenwood groupie. I collected his photos and extracts of his speeches from the local papers and kept them in a scrapbook. I found out where he lived in London and, during one of my summer visits, gazed at his home in Hampstead. I fantasized that he would open the door, his eyes would meet mine, and we would sail off into the sunset. Of course, we would have to deal somehow with his wife. Though, as I didn't want to marry him, being against holy matrimony and the begetting of children, I hoped she wouldn't mind too much.

During the 1954 election campaign, I attended every meeting he addressed that was near enough not to entail a bus fare. Oddly enough, he did notice me and seemed to like my devotion. The chairman usually allowed me to ask a question—there was never an over-abundance of young girls in the audience. The MP for Rossendale evidently was impressed with my grasp of the town planning ideas of his illustrious father Arthur Greenwood, who cropped up rather frequently in my questioning. After one meeting, as the MP passed down the aisle of the hall to the applause of the audience, he actually took hold of my hand as I extended it to shake his. He pulled me after him down the aisle into an anteroom along with the rest of the platform party. "Oh, boy," I thought, it's happening. We're going off into the sunset."

Once in the room, he asked me my name, how old I was, which school I went to, and what I was studying. He then introduced me to the chairman of the meeting, his wife, and sundry other folk before saying quietly to me, "Well, Sophia, you have an unusual name."

"Yes," I replied trembling. Although I was perfectly aware that what this gorgeous man saw before him was a small, pale, skinny teenager dressed in clothes from a jumble sale—though not spotty, I was never spotty—I imagined I saw unusual interest in his eyes. "My sisters are named Michaela, Miranda, and Esther," I feebly added.

"Are you planning a career in politics?" he asked.

"Perhaps," I lied. Actually the idea had never occurred to me, but then I had a wicked thought that I hoped would bring him more under my spell. "I founded a branch of CEWC at my school," I said. "Would you come and speak to us?"

"I'd love to," he said, proving that the spell was working. "But my life is not my own right now. I will have to get my agent to agree to it."

He did manage to come. Naturally, I was the head cook and bottle washer for the event. I was also the Communist candidate in the school's mock election. This was a fact I was not anxious for my hero and potential lover to learn. However, thanks to our darling headmaster, the truth was revealed.

Far from falling back in shock and horror, the MP's interest in me appeared to increase.

"I would like to exchange views with you after the meeting, if you're not rushing home," he said.

Me, rushing home?

True to his word, he stayed behind after the meeting. He questioned me about why I was a Communist and why, having followed him about so faithfully, I was not standing as the Labour candidate? He was very clever. He refrained from rubbishing my views. Rather, he asked me to consider his and whether they were perhaps more realistic and practical. Of course I was spell-bound. I promised to think about it as he kissed me on the forehead and wished me luck—something he would not dare to do today lest he be accused of sexual abuse.

It was just as well that I had already made my final speech in the school election campaign. I doubt I would have been able to present my case with the same fervour as I had before this encounter. As it was, I came in at the bottom of the poll with ten votes; the Conservative candidate won a landslide victory. You would have thought the vote had taken place at

Eton or Harrow instead of in lower middle-class Bacup and Rawtenstall Grammar School, where a good proportion of the fathers were unemployed.

Later on, I received a letter from Tony Greenwood thanking me for my support in his election campaign which he won handsomely. He also invited me to join a group of his constituents in a visit to the House of Commons. As the date coincided with my visit to Rosa, I happily accepted. I have a photograph of me in ankle socks—at age sixteen—standing next to him with his daughter on his other side, on the terrace of the House of Commons, to confirm it. I could not have known how prophetic that visit was to prove of a time when proceedings in Parliament were to control my life.

Later still, when I had recovered from my infatuation with Tony Greenwood, I briefly joined the Communist Party and left it for reasons that had less to do with politics than my becoming involved with another Labour politician. Perhaps I inherited some of my radicalism from my father who could never fit into any political framework. He had to belong to Equity to get work, but he was always late with his subscriptions and when urged by contractors on building sites to join the appropriate union, he would always promise to do so, promises never fulfilled.

On principle, Eli was against whoever was in charge. "He talks through the back of his neck," was his customary summation. He was frequently given his marching orders through the back of someone's neck. Eli's views were based not so much on a philosophy of life than on an attitude. I must admit that I sympathize with some of those views.

What I could not tolerate were his prejudices. He was born long before the age of political correctness. However, I doubt whether it would have affected him much even if he had been a child of the final quarter of the twentieth century. For a radical, Eli Rosen was a dedicated bigot. I could never bear to listen to the radio with him or to be anywhere close to him when he was reading a newspaper. His vehemently expressed opinions on all foreigners, but especially Arabs, or religious leaders and politicians were straight out of *Till Death Us Do Part*, a classic case of someone in a glass house throwing a lot of stones. In Eli's world, only showbiz personalities, and not all of them, were honest and decent and capable of running the country. He became more opinionated as he grew older.

Probably in reaction, my mother spoke of herself as a dyed-in-the-wool, uncompromising Tory, royalist, and patriot. All of which meant that my parents' views really were not that far apart, though neither would have dreamed of acknowledging it. Tolerance was not my parents' forte. Neither was it mine at that stage in my life.

I was not prepared to tolerate their views and could tie them up in knots verbally within minutes of starting an argument. It must have been tiresome for them. It became clear to me that I had to find sparring partners elsewhere. I was more than ready to move on as my headmaster had suggested, though he could have put it more kindly. So when the time came for me to go up to university I almost galloped away.

I would miss my baby sister Esther, whose birth had caused me such anguish.

She was an endearing child—pretty, affectionate, and spoiled by everyone. Because we looked alike, I was frequently taken to be her mother. Later in life, it became a game we both enjoyed playing. She was the only aspect of my home life that I was genuinely sorry to leave behind.

I made a triumphal school exit laden with prizes and scholarships that actually meant real money. For the first time in my life, I had independent means, with some left over that I could send home. I prepared for my new life at Liverpool University with meticulous care. This entailed spending hours in the local library reading the advanced lists of course books, taking notes on their contents, and making lists of all the things I would need to take with me.

At the same time, I came to a momentous decision. I was going to change my name to something less exotic, something that would reflect my Irish and Jewish origins and be less of a conversation starter. After hours of thought, I settled on Sarah.

"From now on," I told my bemused family, "I am to be addressed as Sarah." I spoke as though I was under the influence of Jane Austen. With this adopted speech pattern, I would come out with things like, 'Mama, do you believe the weather warrants the use of a mackintosh?' and 'I should like you to address your letters to Miss Sarah Rosen or it will be embarrassing for me.'

Michaela and Sean fell about with mirth, but practical Miranda pointed out that I was registered at the University as Sophia and it could be confusing.

"For official purposes," I proclaimed. "I will still be known as Sophia. It's what is on my birth certificate and school records, but I will tell all my friends to call me, Sarah and I'll say that's how I'm generally known."

And so I was, except by Esther who could manage neither Sophia nor Sarah due to her lisp. She called me "Fia." Eli persisted with Sophia. He declared that Sarah sounded like a stranger—a somewhat accurate summary, as he and I were more or less strangers. We never really understood one another, a common enough story that makes it all the harder to explain why hardly a day passes without my thinking about him and why, at our mother's funeral, I missed him.

He helped me pack a big, black trunk we bought from a secondhand shop. Into it went my books, my clothes, and a few bits and pieces I had accumulated to make my room in the residence hall more homelike. I also packed my most treasured items that I could not bear to leave behind. Eli asked a friend who had a car to take us to the railway station in Manchester. He kissed me goodbye, reminding me to keep men at arm's length, and neither of us shed a tear. I never lived at home again. My visits were brief and infrequent. I turned my back on my old life with few regrets and without realizing that I would never really cut the ties that bound me to those familiar strangers who were my family.

Michaela was the next to leave home. Within weeks, she had met the man she later married and with whom she lived in mutual adoration for the rest of their lives. Nothing much disturbed her equilibrium. Like my mother, she had the knack of ignoring unpleasant facts as if they did not exist. Only the much later death of our mother really disturbed her. At Mum's funeral, Michaela declared that when Eli died, wild horses would not be able to drag her to his funeral.

Chapter Sixteen

Years later, my sisters and I discussed our lives growing up together. At that distance in time, we concluded that despite the different inadequacies of our parents, we suffered much less damage than psychiatrists would have predicted. The exception was possibly our brother.

I learned a strong sense of self-reliance from those early years. I also learned to watch, observe, and internalize what I saw. From my father, I gained a love of the theatre and the joy of performance.

I shouldn't speak for my siblings, I know. They can tell their own stories. I can only comment on how it seems from my perspective. Michaela was always the closest to my mother. They shared moods and interests—laughing at the same things and blotting out things they found unpleasant. For what it's worth, each was born under the same zodiac sign (Sagittarius) on the same day of the month. They also shared certain characteristics. My mother coped with her difficult life by turning a blind eye to what she didn't want to see. She never allowed doubt to enter her mind and believed that she was the best of all possible mothers. Michaela agreed, while I could not. So, though I loved my mother and felt a lot of compassion for her, we were never close. Michaela disliked our father. After our parents split up, she never saw or spoke to him again.

Miranda felt most at home in the place where circumstances had placed us. She found her security among our neighbours and her school friends. She genuinely loved and was loved in return. She was the local favourite. The people who took her to their bosom referred to me as "the strange and clever one" and to Michaela as the "pretty one." Miranda was, and still is, happiest in the countryside; I remain a committed urbanite. She hardly knew the Stern family and our Jewish ethnicity meant little to her; although later in life, she came closer to it. She learned horse riding, badger trapping, sheep degging, and how to be a good camper. We were so different. I won prizes for writing essays on bird watching without ever watching a bird. I just liked reading about birds, writing essays, and winning prizes. Our sister Miranda speaks with a northeast Lancashire accent to this day and maintains friendships she made in the valley of Rossendale all those years ago.

My brother Sean, though I have never heard a word of complaint or self-pity from him, suffered most from our parents' unhappy marriage. When Sean was eleven, he came home from school and found a note from our mother saying she had left with our youngest sister Esther and would not be returning. She wrote that she would let him know where she was and that she would keep in touch. She felt it was best for him to remain with his father and for Esther, the baby, to go with her. I have imagined the scene of Sean finding the note over and over again. I find it unbearable. She didn't bother to leave a note for Eli.

My brother looks uncannily like the young Jean-Pierre Léaud as he appeared in the Truffaut film *Quatre Cents Coups*. I cannot even think about the film without weeping. I never forgave my mother for this blow to Sean. Whatever pain I felt as a result of the break up of my parents' marriage is centred on this image of my eleven-year-old brother returning from school calling out that he is home. Finding no one there, he reads a note informing him his mother and little sister had left his life. What did this abandoned child do after he had read his mother's message? How many times did he read it? Did he cry? Did he run to tell a neighbour? Or did he simply put down the note and start looking around for something to eat?

What did he say to his father when he returned from work? Did they start planning how they were to cope? Who was to do the shopping, the cooking, the laundry, changing the bed linen?

Or did they just take each day and its chores as it came? Did the boy cry himself to sleep that night or many nights? How did the man react?

One thing I know for sure is our mother made no move to prepare either of them for what she was about to do. She packed secretly, wrote her note, and simply locked up the house before leaving with Esther to catch the coach to London.

I find it extraordinary that my brother continued to love my mother. I have never had the courage to ask him to tell me how he felt that day. Normally, he would come home from football hungry to the smell of cooking, a fire in the grate, and the sound of his mother's voice telling him to drop his muddy football things by the back door. The day she left was not a normal day. He has never complained. He appears to bear no grudge, and I am afraid of upsetting him by probing. Whatever he felt is locked away and out of my reach. I can only imagine his suffering.

For my part, I was less forgiving. Bluntly put, I hated my mother—not for leaving but for the way she left. It was fortunate for my mother that Sean appeared to continue to love her. He has never, to my knowledge, reproached her. He left home to pursue a career in accounting at the earliest opportunity. He remained in close touch with our father sharing his home whenever he returned to Rossendale. Eventually, Sean married a sweet girl whose family knew his story.

During the few years that Esther, the baby, was in the family home, she was loved and pampered by all. I was sixteen when she was born, a most intolerant age. I could not understand how people who were at war with one another could produce a baby. But I adored her when she was born, and we remain close to this day.

Esther was suddenly cut off from her father and brother— we three older girls had already left home—when Miriam took her away to a series of unsatisfactory residential jobs. Miriam finally settled in as a housekeeper, which gave Esther her first really stable home. Curiously enough, the family was Jewish. As Miriam said of that time, "Grandmother Stern," who had passed away some years before, "would have been appalled at the idea of her youngest daughter being someone's housekeeper but would have been comforted to know she was in a Jewish home."

So, this is what I remember of my childhood and our parents—their strengths and especially their weaknesses. Our parents were children when they married and remained children into old age.

Eli muddled through each day never really accepting his life as it had become—a kind of chaos. His real achievement was his children; unfortunately for Eli, this was an achievement he failed to recognize.

Miriam continued to expect and demand. She was proud of her children and depended on us to look after her, which of course we did, even after her second marriage and divorce. Discussions on these lines, which the five of us occasionally have, usually end with someone saying to me,

"But of course, you had Rosa. She loved you best and you were so alike."

Rosa used to call me Thursday's Child who had far to go. My mother called me Rosa's Child. And they were both right. For me, the years following those I have described have been full of events that could not have been foretold. They have included two marriages, one divorce, eight pregnancies, three live births, and life in three different countries. But those years shed no further light, I believe, on why I felt as I did at my mother's funeral. So enough, it is time to put it all to rest.

Part Three: After the Funeral

Chapter Seventeen

The Rosen siblings arrived at the cafeteria attached to Chichester Theatre for a reception arranged in honour of their late mother. Each felt like an understudy rather than the leading actors they considered they should have been following her funeral. Three of the five had little idea what they were doing there.

Sophia, the eldest, had gathered from a brief conversation with their Aunt Alicia that their mother had been in a relationship with an actor based in Chichester, thus accounting for what had seemed like a strange choice of final destination.

She had had little time to digest this information but had considered the reasons for their mother's secrecy. Most likely, it would have been her anticipation of her children's disapproval for taking up with yet another actor after two prior disastrous marriages to actors. Could this Anton have been the love of her mother's life? Ever defensive of her father, Sophia hoped not. But, if Anton had made their mother happy in her last days, she and her siblings should make an effort to be nice to him.

She drew closer to her sister Michaela and whispered, "I think we had better tell the others that we have to go along with whatever happens here. You tell Sean. I'll tell Miranda and Esther."

"What am I supposed to say?" Michaela shot back, clearly not in the best of moods. Whether out of grief for their mother's passing or irritation at the turn of events, Sophia could not tell and now was not the time to probe.

"Just say that because Mum and Anton Dolinsky apparently were an item, we should be nice to him."

"You can be nice to him if that's what you want. He looks the usual poncey type to me, and I just want to get away from this lot as soon as possible," hissed Michaela.

"Please make an effort Michaela. It's only for an hour or so and these people seem to have been genuinely fond of Mum."

Michaela shrugged and moved off to talk to Sean who was receiving condolences from his wife's relatives. Before Sophia could approach Miranda and Esther, her Aunt Alicia detached herself from the Chichester crowd signalling to Sophia that she wanted to talk to her. There was something about Alicia's anxious bustling that slightly alarmed her niece who feared she was about to be faced with yet more surprises.

"Sophia dear," Alicia said in the conspiratorial tone that confirmed Sophia's fears.

"I need to talk to you."

"Good idea," Sophia replied, "but I am not sure now is the best time. I was about to talk to my sisters about being nice to everyone. So can it wait a bit?"

"Well no, love. There's something else I have to tell you before you speak to them. It will only take a minute."

Sophia nodded obediently as her aunt took her arm and drew her aside.

"It's just that Anton and the folk here have organized a kind of celebration of your mother's life that I thought you should know about. They've made a film. I haven't seen it, but they asked me for some photos, family videos, and what have you. I believe they even contacted your father. It will probably be very professional and nice for you, but I thought you should not be taken by surprise. That's all."

That's all? Sophia took a moment to digest what she had just heard and then she asked,

"They won't be asking for audience participation will they?"

"What do you mean?" Alicia asked, her eyes darting around the assembled crowd. Most hovered around tables laden with food appearing uncertain as to whether or not they were invited to eat or should wait for some kind of signal.

"I mean will any of us be asked to say anything? If so, I feel we should have been prepared in advance. I don't think any of us would be happy to have it land on us especially when we're all feeling upset and not a little confused."

Sophia's tone was cold and Alicia, who was close to her niece and was unaccustomed to the reception she was receiving, felt it.

"Don't worry darling," she said. "I think it's all been organized for your benefit as much as anything. You won't be asked to do a thing, I'm sure."

Further conversation was brought to a halt by an announcement,

"Before we begin the programme that has been created in honour of the life of Miriam Stern Rosen, you are invited to help yourselves to refreshments, to take a seat, and to make yourselves comfortable. In doing so, we, a group of Miriam's friends from the Chichester and other theatres, would like to express our condolences to her sister, Alicia, and to her children and their families. We grieve with them in their loss and very much hope that what follows will bring them comfort and some very happy memories."

Alicia squeezed Sophia's arm. "It will be fine, you'll see," she said.

Sophia had always regarded Alicia as the practical down-to-earth aunt, utterly trustworthy and full of common sense. The eldest of the three Stern sisters and the most stable, she was the least complex and had always been the "fixer" and the "shoulder to lean on." For the first time in her life, Sophia wondered if, in the matter of the arrangements of Miriam's departure from this earth, Alicia had gone too far. Surely, it would have been appropriate to consult Miriam's children. As it was, Sophia found herself facing three pairs of enquiring eyes in which she could detect more than a trace of hostility.

"What's all this about?" Miranda asked as they helped themselves to the buffet. "Did you know about it?"

"I received a heavy hint from Alicia a few minutes ago. She assures me we'll enjoy it."

"I'm intrigued," Esther murmured to her sisters as she helped herself to the smoked salmon. "Have you noticed no meat or shellfish? Very thoughtful. Little did they know there was no need to bother."

Esther moved on toward Sean and his family but, as she did so, Sean detached himself from the group and came toward his older three sisters.

"I think we ought to circulate," he said. "These people have gone to some trouble it seems, so we should be nice to them."

"You're right," Sophia replied. "Let's each take our food to a table where there are people we don't know."

"What for?" Michaela objected. "May I remind you that we are at our mother's funeral not a cocktail party? I don't feel much like socializing. Actually, I would leave right now if I could. I've had enough." With that said, she took her plate of food and headed for an empty window seat.

"I'll go with her," Miranda said. "We can't let her sit on her own."

Sophia, dutiful as ever, shrugged and joined a table occupied by Anton Dolinsky and a few other people she assumed to be part of the "Chichester crowd."

Alicia was already looking comfortably settled at a neighbouring table when Sean joined her.

And so it was, that when the presenter called for silence and the curtains were pulled across the windows as lights were dimmed, the Rosen siblings were scattered around the room. With the exception of Michaela and Miranda, they were unable to communicate with one another about what followed.

It was the story of their mother's life, a story which, from time to time, they were able to recognize. The presentation was accompanied by excerpts from the operas she was said to have appeared in. There were still photographs of Miriam as a child and as a rather glamorous teenager. A photograph of her in costume was accompanied by a rather scratchy recording of her singing *The Moon and I*. This was followed by a home movie of her wedding to Eli Rosen. She looked incredibly childlike; he was the dashing and debonair bridegroom with sleeked back hair and a small moustache in the manner of Ronald Colman.

These images were followed by jerky clips of movies featuring the children. Many were acutely embarrassing to the adult siblings—especially one showing Sean as a baby peeing in the bath. These were children who seemed never to have grown up, since the years of their maturity were not recorded, neither was the divorce from their father. The Michael Katz years may as well not have occurred.

Miriam mysteriously and, it had to be said, graciously passed from being a radiant young mother surrounded by a brood of happy children, to being an equally radiant partner to Anton Dolinsky. Pictures showed her accompanying him to various opening nights, other people's weddings, and a bar mitzvah wearing outfits her children had never seen or knew she possessed. This part of the presentation was clearly more professional than the prior images.

The programme ended with a short tribute to Miriam by Anton. He focused on how privileged he was to have known her and how much he would miss her. He also said how sorry he was not to have known her when she was a brilliant young singer and the devoted mainstay of a brood of talented children. He concluded by saying it had been her dying wish that he be the custodian of her ashes until such time as they could be mingled with his.

Dry-eyed Sophia was in shock and wanted nothing more than to make an exit with her brother and sisters to discuss what they had just seen and heard. Their mother had remained a mystery not only to her but to her entire family. As the eldest, she knew she should be extending thanks, but she could not.

If she spoke out, she was certain to say something no one wanted to hear. In time, she knew she would be happy that their mother, who had led such a hard, disappointing life, had found some glamour in its last phase. But for the moment, her entire being was filled with anger. She was angry with her mother for cutting them all so completely out of her life that they could not know she had finally been happy. She was angry that Miriam had brought her lifelong habit of denial to such a pitch and she was angry on behalf of her father.

At the same time, she recognized that this anger was not entirely rational. She would calm down. For the time being, it was best to say nothing except grateful platitudes to the Chichester people. She had noticed that at the end of the film, there was a pause while it was collectively decided that applause was inappropriate and Anton was openly weeping. As she rose to take her leave, she paused to touch his arm. "Thank you," she said. "That was really beautiful. As you know, I live abroad, but I would like to give you my card in case you feel like keeping in touch."

He stood up to embrace her, "Thank you. I'd like that."

"We have to be getting back," she said. "Please express our thanks to everyone involved." She moved to the next table to kiss Alicia and Sean. "Don't say a word," her brother whispered to her. "It was a fairy tale ending just like the beginning and nothing much happened in between."

"We'll talk," Sophia said. "Now I must gather up the girls."

Chapter Eighteen

It turned out that none of them wanted to go their separate ways, so it was hastily decided that they would return to London together in the funeral car. Sean bade farewell to his puzzled wife and her family explaining that he needed to spend a little more time with his sisters.

After ten minutes of heavy silence, Esther was the first to speak.

"Did any of you have any idea that Mum went to all those affairs and had those clothes, not to mention a lover?"

Michaela, close to tears, snapped back, "She was entitled to her own version, wasn't she?"

"Nobody's denying her that Michaela," Sophie quickly returned. "I think the problem is that so much was left out. I don't begrudge her whatever happiness she found with Anton and his crowd. What hurts is that she didn't share it with any of us and, apparently, couldn't be honest about her history with someone who is now in charge of her remains."

"What do you think he's going to do with them? And don't make jokes about it, Michaela," Miranda shot at her sister.

"If you think I'm in a joking mood, Miranda, you don't know much about me, do you?"

"Sorry," Miranda humbly replied, forestalling another angry outburst from her clearly distressed sister.

"What do any of us really know about each other?" Sean spoke for the first time. "We think we do, but we don't really."

"That's getting a bit deep darling and I'm not sure that I am up to any more soul-searching today," Michaela said.

"All the same," Sophia responded, "after what we've just witnessed, Sean makes a good point. It seems we really didn't know our mother. Are we supposed to leave it like that? Maybe some soul-searching is called for. Don't we want to know each other better?"

"I'm not sure," Esther took her eldest sister's hand. "I'm afraid we might end up hurting one another. For instance, I can tell you what I feel now, but I can't promise you that I will remember how I feel now in twenty years time. And if I tell you how I feel now, each one of you will remember it differently. That's how family myths are built up and once they become folklore, there's no changing it."

"Jesus," Michaela retorted. "One cremation and you're all philosophers."

"Michaela, please," Sophie pleaded. "This wasn't any old cremation. It was our farewell to our mother, a woman who seems to have been a different person to different people. My memory of her is quite clearly different than yours.

"As you said when we were on our way here, you were closest to her. She loved you best you said. But you didn't know any of this Anton stuff."

"She might have loved me best Sophia, but she admired you, the great achiever, so confident, afraid of nothing, getting whatever you wanted. Daddy's and Rosa's pet."

"I don't think so, Michaela. You are just proving Sean's point. Yes I've had my successes—but afraid of nothing? You're absolutely wrong. And are you sure our mother admired me? It seemed to me she was puzzled by me. But never mind. It's water under the bridge. Today is a day for being honest with one another."

"Well," Michaela pursued, "it seemed to me you were afraid of nothing while I was full of fears."

Miranda snorted, "You! Full of fears? Full of bullshit is more like it."

"Don't start," Sean practically shouted. "It gets us nowhere."

"I was afraid of our father for some time," Michaela spoke softly.

Four pairs of eyes stared at Michaela. Sophia was the first to speak, "Afraid of him?" Is that why you hate him?"

"Maybe. Who knows where it started. I didn't even meet him until I was five. He was gone after I was conceived and remained absent until he returned from entertaining the troops and killing the Japanese or whatever he said he was doing. But I do remember that everyone was talking about peace. It seemed to me that peace wasn't in our house. Our father's homecoming destroyed a nice existence—just me, Sophia, our mother, and a few other kids from time to time."

"But Michaela," Sophia protested, "You can't blame our father for that. Our mother, like thousands of other women, had to make adjustments when her husband returned after a long absence. Maybe she couldn't do it."

The three younger siblings held their tongues. They had no memory of the time their sisters were discussing.

"Whatever," Michaela sighed. "I can only tell you what I remember—I had a happy childhood until Mr. X appeared on the scene. Don't you remember Sophia, how he wouldn't let me bring Billy the cat into the house? The poor thing had to stay in the cold passage. He told me it wasn't healthy to kiss and cuddle a cat, so he dragged Billy off me."

"I remember the cat," Sophia confirmed. "You called him Boo Boo, dressed him up like a doll, and pushed him around in your doll's pram. You also, as I recall, put him in the oven to dry after you bathed him."

This caused the others to laugh.

"I did not," Michaela protested. "I loved that cat. Anyway, our father also threw me out of my mother's bed."

"Oh, for Christ's sake, Michaela," Miranda joined in. "What did you expect? You were five years old; you shouldn't have been in your mother's bed anyway. That was where our father belonged. If that's why you hate him, you're old enough to realize the error of your ways."

"What's that supposed to mean? Anyway, you've no reason to take his side. From what I've been told, he was not too happy that he was presented with yet another daughter."

"That's a really mean thing to say Michaela. Who told you that?"

"You did tell me once, you know, that you felt no one loved you when you were a child," Sean told his sister.

"Well," Miranda admitted, "that's no reason for Michaela to repeat something she said she heard about my father not wanting me."

"That's not what I said. I said he was not too happy to have another daughter.

"He wanted a son, you said."

"Please," Sophia intervened. "Let's not insult each other. Most men want a son and next time around our father got one."

"Do you know what I remember about you being born Miranda?" Michaela asked.

"No, but I think you're going to tell me."

Michaela ignored the sarcasm and continued. "When my mother told me she was having another baby, I asked her, "So where does that put me?"

"And that's how it all began," Esther spoke, making her first contribution to this conversation with a heavy sigh. She was clearly concerned about the testy relationship between two of her sisters. Her intervention caused a much-needed pause in the exchanges as each of the siblings considered what had been said.

The funeral car was making its way through heavy traffic toward the London-bound motorway. For Sophia, the exiled Brit, the landscape that the others found boring gave her a nostalgic feeling. It was so different from the suburbs of San Francisco. Everything here was on a much smaller scale; it was greener, quieter, and cosier. After all, this was her home. However far she travelled, her roots were here. She had lived in places where she didn't know the language, but she had always managed with English and found fellow Brits. She had never been conscious of being homesick. Nevertheless, there were cultural differences even in America; San Francisco is as English feeling as one is likely to get. It took this journey home for her mother's funeral to remind her of where she really belonged. It was good to be with her sisters and her brother and, to some extent, to reconnect.

Sophia broke the silence by saying,

"I remember all of you being born. And I don't recall ever asking myself where that put me, Michaela. I think I knew, practically from birth, that I had a special responsibility as the eldest, to be well, responsible.

Maybe that was my problem. I was never really a proper child, if you know what I mean."

"You were certainly more like a mother than a sister to me," Esther said.

"Maybe that's why you've always been so bloody serious. You always had your head in a book—a bit of a party pooper really." Michaela added.

"Actually, we're all a bit like that, aren't we?" Sean asked.

"Speak for yourself brother." This came from Miranda. "I'm always up for a good bash."

"Me too," Michaela added.

"I don't believe it. Something they agreed on!" voiced Esther as she suddenly slipped out of her safety belt, stood up, and kissed Michaela and Miranda, then turned to include Sean and Sophia before she sat down.

"You couldn't do that in a regular car," noted Sean who seemed to be a bit embarrassed at this display of sisterly love.

"You know, Sophia," Michaela said after a further moment of silence between them all, "despite what I said about you being too intense or whatever, I really admired you through-out our childhood. I still do, for that matter. You were so good at everything from school to lighting that horrible fire we had in Edgeside. I should have resented you, I suppose, but I never did. The neighbours called you the clever one and me the pretty one, which actually suited me. I had no claims to being clever and couldn't care less."

"What did they call me?" asked Miranda curiously.

"Too late for your dinner, I should think."

"Michaela, that was one of our dad's jokes. Do you realise that?"

"Was it Sophia? It just came into my head. Actually Miranda, I think you were known as the sporty one because you were always up on the farms milking or degging or whatever you called it."

"Sporty, like one of the Spice Girls. I didn't know that. But I do remember spending a lot of time outside the home. I was always going for what the kids these days call sleepovers. I guess I just wanted to get away from home. I hated all the quarrelling about money and who had smoked all the ciga- rettes. I must say, it seemed to me that I was loved more outside my home than in it."

"You were always much more of a local girl than the rest of us," Sophia told her.

"I had a lot of friends in the neighbourhood and still do as a matter of fact."

"That makes two of us," Sean said. "But in my case, it's largely down to Debs who still has family there."

"But you were there long after the rest of us had left," Michaela remarked. It seemed as if she was going to con- tinue, but she suddenly stopped, aware, no doubt, that she might have wandered into sensitive territory. But Sean took the lead she had offered.

Chapter Nineteen

"You mean after Mum left and Dad and I were on our own? Yes, as a matter of fact, I do have one friend in particular from those days. His family were very good to me when— well when Dad and I were a bit lost. Trevor's mum made meals for us and did some ironing and things. Trev and I were in the Scouts together and on the school football team. We're still very close."

"That's nice," Sophia said. "Sean darling, do say if you don't want to talk about it, but I have long wanted to ask you about that time. I know we wrote to one another, but I always tried not to upset you any further. How did you cope?"

"And," added Miranda, "what were your feelings about Mum?"

Sean sighed. "I suppose today, the day of her funeral is as good a time to tell you as any. Frankly, I don't know what I would have done without Dad. That's why I get upset, Michaela, when I hear you, and I heard Mum at times, calling him Mr. X like he's a nonperson or a wicked one. It was hard for him too, you know, to be left to run a house and care for an eleven-year-old son."

As the car laboured its way through heavy traffic and the now torrential rain, Sean paused. It seemed to his sisters that he was deciding what and how much to confide in them. When he resumed, he was in control. "I don't think any of you know that I've had a long period of therapy."

The sisters shook their heads but did not interrupt.

"I didn't do it until after I was married. Deborah encouraged me. She could see how much what had happened still troubled me. At first, I dismissed the idea as so much crap, but I have to admit it has helped. I don't think I ever actively blamed our mother, but I was very hurt by what she did. I couldn't help feeling that I was somehow to blame. For instance, if I had been a better scholar, she would not have been disappointed in me and she wouldn't have left."

"Oh, darling," Sophia murmured, her eyes filled with tears, as she leaned across and took her brother's hand.

"Don't Sophia," he said. "I'm fine now, really. I don't want any of you to get upset. It's all in the past. It is history, and I moved on long ago. Sybil, my therapist, helped me to look my story in the face. She made me realize I was not to blame. I also came to understand that, given their situation and their characters, neither were my parents. My mother must have been desperate to leave her only son. No one can know how things would have been if there was enough money or if Dad had more work on a regular basis.

"Maybe they should never have married. Maybe they should have had fewer children. But maybe you could say the same about half the marriages in the world."

As he paused for breath, Michaela said, "I think the therapy made you too kind Sean."

"At least it didn't make him one-sided," Miranda retorted.

"Just let him tell it how he sees it," Esther said. "Go on Sean."

"Okay, here's what happened. I came home from school one Monday afternoon after football practice. Hungry and muddy, I found the back door locked. The front door always was locked. It was used only for the ambulance man who came to take me to have stitches or my leg in plaster or something—oh, and when Mum went into labour with Esther. The back door was never locked, so I knew something had happened. I went to our next door neighbour who had a son my age and with whom we were very friendly. Mrs. Woodstock gave me a funny look and asked if I'd like a cup of tea. This was not her usual response to my knock on her door. She told me she had the key to our door and asked if I'd like her to come in with me. This was also very strange. I said no to both offers because I wanted to get into the house to see what was going on.

"I found the note from Mum telling me she had gone away with Esther and would not be coming back. She said she loved me and would let me know where she was in a little while. My dinner was in the oven.

"I read it a few times looking, I think, for some clue as to what I had done wrong. But that was all it said. And there was no note for Dad, who, that day at least, had some work and was still out. I don't think I really believed the note. I was well accustomed to our parent's rows and threats and storming out of the house. But they had always come back.

"So, at that point, I didn't cry. I locked the back door because I didn't want Mrs. Woodstock or Mum's friend Florrie, or any of my mates coming in just then. I washed my hands and ate my dinner and, since no one was around to stop me, I took a carton of ice cream out of our little fridge and ate half of it. Then I got out my homework.

"It was only when I started to try to write an essay on "A Major Event in My Life" did I go over Mum's note again, and then I started to cry. I was still crying when Dad came home and found the back door locked.

"I will always remember his first words, 'Have you been crying son? Big boys don't cry.' I showed him the note and he didn't shed a tear.

'Don't worry son,' he said. 'We'll manage. Your mother has left the house but, as far as I am concerned, she's been gone for years.'"

Sean paused for a moment before continuing, "I remember wondering if that was that as far as he was concerned, but what about me? Did he not think I needed a mother and I would miss her? And what about my little sister? Wasn't he sad that she had gone?

"I cried a lot in the weeks that followed but only when Dad was not there or couldn't hear. We were managing and I didn't want to make it harder for him. We ate out a lot. I made the breakfast and, when we were home, he fixed dinner. I was worried about having clean shirts and sports gear for school. Sometimes, when I didn't want to trouble Trevor's Mum again, I washed things at night and put them on still damp in the morning. Dad paid a neighbour to do some cleaning and to change the bed linen, but the house never looked the same as when Mum was there. Nothing was the same.

"Dad did his best and I loved him for it. But nothing could make up for the loneliness I felt when he was out performing in his shows or the pain I endured when I had to tell people that I had no mother. It was easier than telling the truth that I had a mother somewhere—but I didn't know where or if I'd ever see her again."

By this time, all the sisters, even Michaela, were rummaging for tissues.

"At last," Sean continued, "after about six months, she wrote. In her letter, she explained that she had tried a few times to write but it was hard to word it in a way I would understand. She had stayed with her sister Rosa for a bit before looking for a job where she could also take Esther. The first position was no good, so she moved on to what became a worse situation. But now she was with a nice family looking after their children and doing some cooking. Esther was in a good school. She provided a telephone number where I could call her. She also mentioned that I could visit when she was more settled and I had saved the fare. The number was a London exchange, which seemed like another world to me at the time, but at least I knew she was alive and had somewhere to live, somewhere I could call. She told me not to tell Dad she had written and on no account to give him the number.

Things became easier after that, for me at least. I think Dad noticed I'd cheered up, but he asked no questions. He was busy with a new pantomime at that time.

"People were kind to me, especially at school, but I decided, when the time came, that I did not want to stay on. I figured Eli would find life easier if he did not have to look after me. I would follow my older sisters and leave home.

"Sophia, you were doing postgraduate studies at LSE. Michaela was married and Miranda was living with someone she'd met at work. None of you had been home since Mum left. Sophia wrote regularly, Miranda less often, and Michaela not at all."

Sean paused, "Do you want me to continue? It did get better."

"Only if you want to," Sophia said. "Personally, I think it's good for us to hear."

"Okay, when I was ten I was part of a family of seven—mother, father, three older sisters, me, and a little sister. When I was eleven, I had only my father, or so it seemed to me at the time. I can say now that I never really lost you. After the break, we gradually regrouped and added to the numbers as we all had married and had children of our own.

"Our mother was remarried for a time. That's when I saw her again. I had joined the Royal Navy as a trainee accountant. At the first opportunity, I phoned her and we arranged to meet.

She invited me to her home at a time when Michael, the new husband, would not be in. At first, I thought that maybe she hadn't told him she had a son. If I hadn't wanted to see her so much I might have decided not to go.

"But then I realized that she knew this would be a very emotional reunion. She thought it better held just between the two of us, and she was right. We both cried. She told me how she had hated leaving me like she did. If she waited to say goodbye, she knew she would never have been able to leave, and she deemed it best for everyone that she did. She knew I would be alright with Eli who, at any rate, deserved to have one of his children with him. I never asked her, not then and not ever, why she didn't talk things through with our Dad to arrange a mutually acceptable parting. I did not want to expose her, especially not just then.

"You may not want to hear this, and maybe I shouldn't say it now she is dead, but the fact is our mother was a moral coward. She ran away from things that upset her or that she feared. Once our dentist refused to treat me because "Mrs. Rosen" had failed repeatedly to turn up for appointments she desperately needed if she were not to lose her remaining teeth.

"Miranda, you once told me she refused to have breast scans or blood tests. She just did not want to know. And she couldn't face having it out with our father. It was easier to just go. It was just the way she was."

Sean sighed and added, "You know, I've wanted to tell all this to you for a very long time. I never had the opportunity. Even now, I feel I've being going on too much."

Sophia was the first to speak. "Thank you darling. That couldn't have been easy for you. I must say, I have been much less forgiving of our mother than you have."

"Don't we know it," Michaela's tone announced that she was ready to do battle on Miriam's behalf. "You could never see what a tyrant our father was. He forced his theatricals on us all and expected Mum to keep house on thin air."

Quiet to this point, Esther explained, "He was never a tyrant Michaela. Whatever his faults, that's going too far. Listen to what Sean said. How many men would have just got on with things like he did after suddenly losing half his family?"

"It's all very well for you, Esther," Michaela replied. "You were too young to know what was going on. You never had to suffer the humiliation of being in one of his rotten shows, listening to him going on as if he were Sir Ralph Richardson."

"You're hopeless, Michaela. You exaggerate everything. You may not have liked being in his shows. I wasn't too keen either. Anyway, I seem to recall that you had several goes at humiliating him."

"Miranda, are you referring to what I did when Sophia and I played the part of Rudolf the red-nosed reindeer? If anything has been exaggerated, that has. That has become a family myth."

"Are you saying it never happened?"

"Anyway, I love that story Michaela," interceded Esther. "I think you were very smart."

"And how," Sophia added. "You don't know the half of how clever Michaela was as a child. She got out of doing anything she didn't like doing by pretending she couldn't do it."

"Well, I didn't bloody get out of being in his so-called shows."

"Our Dad was an actor, Michaela, a show man. What did you want from him?" Sean asked, speaking for the first time since he explained how life had been for him. He had withdrawn when he had finished, perhaps regretting he had said as much as he had.

"Oh Sean, come on. He wanted to be a famous actor. He was, and still is, living in a fantasy world. He has spent his life performing in front of people who wouldn't recognize a proper theatre if they fell over it."

"You're a hard case, Michaela," Sophia sounded close to tears. "If anyone lived in a fantasy world, it was the woman we've just dispached to the next life. What do you say about that film the Chichester folk made?"

"There's no way she could have had anything to do with that. Anyway, we're discussing Mr. X not Mum."

"Will you ever make your peace with him?" Miranda asked her sister.

"Perhaps. When he apologizes to me for what I had to go through as a child and that will be never."

"You make him sound like such an ogre, Michaela." Sophia persisted. "He was never violent. He did his best to keep us all. He was actually very entertaining when he was in the mood."

"What about all the sulks? Months of not talking to our mother. Sending notes wanting to know what she'd done with his socks."

"But Michaela, Mum also gave him the silent treatment. She also wrote notes. We all hated it, but you can't put all the blame on Eli."

"Okay, Sean, I get it. I understand where you're coming from. But you also didn't have to take part in his shows.

Whatever else I have managed to wipe out from my child-hood, I cannot forget those bloody shows. Do you know, I used to pray that the concert hall would burn down with no one in it so that Jack and the effing Beanstalk or whatever he was doing that year had to be cancelled. How would you like to have been dressed up as a sunflower or a genie in a bottle or the back half of a reindeer who, apparently that year to fit in with the current song for Christmas, accosted Little Red Riding Hood instead of the wolf?

Don't laugh Esther. I actually had a few sessions with a psychiatrist to get rid of Christmas nightmares."

"You're kidding."

"No, Miranda, I am not. Rudolf the red-nosed reindeer haunted my dreams for years. In fact, he played a bigger part in my nightmares then he did in Mr. X's pantomime. I do have to admit that the psychiatrist and I ended up roll-ing around with laughter, not the usual outcome of a session with what our dear father called a 'trick cyclist.' Actually, that about sums him up."

Seeing that Michaela was rather relishing the telling of her tale and had clearly lightened up, Esther begged her to tell the Rudolf story.

"You're getting me at it you wicked girl. But alright. So-phia was the front half of the stupid animal and I was its bum. This meant I had to be bent double in a stuffy costume for hours on end."

Seeing Sophia raise her eyebrows at this bit, Michaela corrected herself,

"Well, okay, half an hour. Anyway, we had to learn a dance and come on the stage while the band played that terrible song. I had to try to coordinate my leg movements with Sophia's and wag the animal's tail. I think it had a tail. I was bloody hopeless. I kept kicking Sophia's legs and forgetting to wag the frigging tail. I got Sophia to show Father a picture of a reindeer proving that no tail was to be seen but, of course, he had an answer for it. Rudolf was a mythical creature loosely based on a reindeer and could be invested with all manner of additional body parts as well as a passion for carrots—another bit of business that was part of the act. Sophia handled that bit and was superb, needless to say.

"Eli played a character of some sort who had a long scene with Rudolf that called for alternately feeding him carrots and making him cry. During this scene, Sophia had to squeeze a bottle with tubes and water leading to the eyes to make tears and manipulate a switch behind the creature's eyes to make them light up with joy. As you can imagine, Sophia had all the interesting bits.

"I did everything I could to get out of being Rudolf's hind quarters. I even complained it made me dizzy so I couldn't get my tail to wag. All to no avail. I appealed to our mother; I turned on the water works in front of the rest of the cast. I even farted repeatedly inside the costume so Sophia would protest. But she just told me off in private to keep me out of trouble.

"Finally, on the last night of the actual performance, I walked backward off the stage when we should have been moving forward. It earned a huge laugh from the audience, but our father was furious. 'What kind of a trouper are you?' he yelled at me. 'No daughter of mine should ever do a thing like that, last night or no last night.'"

Michaela continued speaking, "You have no idea what this did to me apart from my nightmares. Eli, Mr. X, never used me in his shows again. And it was the first time, at the age of ten or thereabouts, that I wondered if I was his daughter. It would explain a lot if I wasn't. Have I told you that my blood group is not the same as any of yours?

"All of you and our mother are B positive. I'm O. I never dared asked her what it meant. Now, I'll never know. I'm certainly not going to ask Mr. X."

"I'd get your blood tested again if I were you," Miranda advised. "They can make mistakes you know."

"And what you are saying," Esther added "is that our mother had a lover while Dad was away."

"Let's not go there." For once, Sean sounded like he wanted to assert authority on the discussion.

"Sean's right," Sophia said. "I personally don't think there can be any doubt about your paternity, Michaela. I don't really know what the blood test evidence indicates, even if it is accurate. I would have remembered if there was anyone else in Mum's life before you were born, and I definitely do not. Your hatred of Dad can't all be due to Rudolf. Don't you think it's more to do with taking Mum's side in the separation?"

"Possibly," Michaela admitted. "But I was talking about how it started and I don't see anything changing now. I haven't spoken to Eli Rosen in years."

"It's a pity, Michaela. In my view, you both lose out." Sean quietly said.

Chapter Twenty

As the car reached the outskirts of London, the rain eased off leaving curtains of splashes on the shop windows and reflections of light in the puddles on the pavements. The light was beginning to fade. Perhaps this reminded Sophia that this valuable time with her siblings, not to be repeated in the foreseeable future, was drawing to an end. And so she suggested,

"Why don't we get the driver to drop us all at my hotel so we can continue to talk for a bit longer over coffee? Can you make it?"

"I'd have to call home," Esther said. "I'm already later than I'd said I'd be."

"We'll all have to call home," Michaela added. "But I think Sophia's idea is a good one. God knows when we'll have another chance to be together and talk. It is quite interesting, isn't it?"

No one dissented as they all pulled out cell phones while Sophia gave instructions to the driver. She was staying at the Sherlock Holmes Hotel in Baker Street. She had responded to a gibe from Michaela about her reputed taste for grand hotels by saying, "Modest but very conveniently situated."

When they eventually arrived at the hotel, the driver was thanked by all for his assistance. Sophia then instructed her siblings to make themselves comfortable in the coffee lounge while she collected her room key from reception. On the way to her room to drop off her coat, she asked a waiter to take their orders and to bring a pot of mint tea for her.

Actually, she was buying a bit of time for herself. She was deciding whether or not to confide in her siblings the real reason she had chosen to stay at the Sherlock Holmes. At one time, she had worked in a public relations office nearby, and it was in this hotel that she had had a very distressing encounter with someone who was to become a major part of her life. As the rest was now history, she decided not to men-

151

tion it to the others. It would be a diversion from the matters of the day.

When she rejoined them, she was pleased to see that Esther, for once, was holding the floor. This was apparently in response to something Michaela had said about her being the spoiled youngest child.

Esther held her own, "How can you say that? Okay, maybe for a few years. I was the baby and everyone petted me but look what happened next. Do you think for one moment that I wasn't damaged by what happened? I was six-years-old and suddenly I had no father, no brother, and I was the nuisance kid of somebody's housekeeper. For God's sake, if I had been spoiled up to then, believe me, it all stopped. I didn't understand anything. Our mother didn't spend much time explaining it to me."

"That must have been tough for you," Miranda conceded, "but you weren't the only one, and to be honest, we all seem to have come out of it alright."

"In that, you have to speak for yourself," Esther said quickly. "If that's how you feel, I'm happy for you. As far as I'm concerned, the pain never really goes away, does it Sean?"

"I'd like to change the subject, if you don't mind," her brother replied. "It's all in the past and as Miranda says, we're not doing too badly. Things could have turned out a lot worse."

"Hear, hear. That's my boy." This time it was Michaela who spoke. "There's no point in going over things. I know who's to blame. I've got a clear conscience and I just get on with my life."

Sophia had been standing listening to these exchanges and now seated herself next to Esther. "But love, isn't that why we're sitting here to go over a few things we have never discussed? It may be a long time before we have another opportunity. Esther was talking about the pain she still feels. It might help her to talk about it to the few people who understand what it's all about."

"But we're not therapists, Sophia and I believe that people who bury their past and don't keep going on about it are healthier than those who live it over and over. Anyway, what are we talking about? Our mother upped and left just like thousands of women all over the world every day of the week. At the end of the day it's no big deal."

"Michaela," Esther sighed in exasperation. "I see damaged people every day in my work and, believe me, their greatest need is to talk. And I would like to talk now. Not for long, just for a minute to try to make you understand what it was like for me to go from being the adored youngest child into a series of strange homes and different schools.

"When we finally settled down, I could stay at the same school for more than one term. I also started receiving letters from Sophia. Then my mother started up with that horrible Michael, and I felt like I was all alone again. So when you start mocking my devotion to my boys and go on about how spoiled I was and my bourgeois existence, do try to understand that I am busy compensating."

"We know you are a wonderful mother and I'm not aware of anyone mocking you."

"You don't see it Sophia, because you're not here. I may have missed out on education, but I'm not stupid. I see the looks that fly around when I call home and the smirks when I talk about Shamanism and New Age Music."

"Guilty, as usual," Michaela piped up. "I'm sorry, Esther. I can't help it. I do think all that alternative stuff is crap. But honestly, if it works for you, I promise to keep my views to myself."

"Don't patronize her, Michaela. I happen to know how Esther feels," said Miranda. "You are always very sniffy about my collectables, dismissing them as dust collectors. I can't say that they compensate for the years I spent without a real home. My compensation was David. God knows where I would be today if I hadn't met him."

"On the front page of the *Sun* I should think," Michaela laughed. Have you ever told Sophia about all your adventures with pop stars and Asian cooks?"

"Don't exaggerate. The pop star wasn't a star at the time. He was just one of dozens of Liverpool wannabes. And yes,

I wrote almost everything to Sophia and I told absolutely everything to Sean, didn't I brother?"

"Yes. It was quite entertaining. The excitement went out of my life when you married David."

"At least you get to eat free in one of several restaurants," chided Michaela.

"Is the business doing well, Miranda?" Sophia asked. She wasn't quite sure whether she was sorry or glad that the conversation had taken a lighter note. She was actually quite worried about Esther whose revelations appeared to be genuine and unfinished. She was determined to spend time with her youngest sister before returning home to San Francisco.

"Didn't you know?" Michaela asked. "Miranda is our rich sister. There are articles about her and David all over the place. They are Gordon Ramsay and Jamie Oliver all rolled into one."

"Mostly due to David and his parents," Miranda said. "They have been marvellous. And, of course, we couldn't have done it if we'd had children. We've had to be totally committed. It's a demanding business though it's a bit easier now."

"Do you wish you'd had children?" Esther asked.

"Of course. But I'm not complaining. If I hadn't had to have a hysterectomy I'd never have met David. You know we met in the patients' recovery lounge at the hospital, Sophia?"

"Yes, you told me."

"That was the subject of a *How They Met* thing in one of the Sundays"

"Do you still have that Sean? I'd like to see it."

"I'll look at home, Sophia. Maybe."

"Well," Sophia sighed after a minute. "I'm not sure, with all that talk, we are any closer to understanding our mother. That film really bothered me."

"I'll probably be the first to be able to ask her all about it."

It was Sean who spoke. The girls looked at him and then at one another, their faces registering various degrees of shock.

"What do you mean?" Miranda finally asked.

"I wasn't sure whether to tell you today. Deborah didn't want me to. I've got colon cancer. She saw my notes—incurable and inoperable."

The tears that had been more or less held back throughout this long day, now streamed out of four pairs of eyes.

"Oh, Lord," Sean said. "I shouldn't have told you."

"Why not? We'd have known sooner or later. So why not sooner?"

"Michaela's right," Sophia said. "You mustn't accept it Sean. I mean, this 'incurable' business. I know loads of people who've made it through colon cancer. There are new types of treatments, and the sooner you start on something the better."

"Don't you think I haven't tried some of them? The result is it is spreading."

"And you haven't said anything to any of us? Oh Sean, we might have been able to help."

"How Miranda? I didn't want to upset the whole family especially now when Mum has died."

"Does Dad know?"

"No. Only Deb and now you."

"Well, she shouldn't have told you what it said in the notes."

"We agreed it was our problem to deal with and to be open with one another, Esther."

"And I'll tell you why that was wrong Sean. You may all scoff at this, but it has been proven that there is a psychological aspect to cancer—actually to all illnesses, but cancer is included. It helps to think positively and to receive therapy to strengthen you to do it. There's a whole clinic devoted to it. People who were diagnosed to be terminal have walked out of there alive. It's worth a go, Sean. I'll send you the details."

"I suppose it's worth looking in to."

"I'm upset with you, Sean." Michaela intervened. "You let me go on about Mr. X, all of us talking rubbish, while all the time you are sick. That is rather more important than what we remember and what we don't."

"I told you, I didn't intend to say anything. Not today anyway. It just came out because of us wanting to find out about our mother."

Miranda moved closer to her brother and put her arm through his. "Don't be so worried," he said. "I feel fine. I can hardly believe what the doctors tell me. To tell you the truth, the treatment I've had makes me feel worse, and I can't eat. But now, it's as if nothing is wrong with me. This could go on for ages. I'm really sorry about what I said about being the first to see Mum."

"You can be wrong. Any one of us could be run over or fall down stairs or whatever at any time."

Sophia, who had been silent after her first reaction to her brother's news, gave a deep sigh. "That's right, Michaela. But, in any case, it doesn't matter whether we ever find out what really went on in our mother's life. When it comes to things like this, the truth about the past really doesn't matter.

"When you think about it, there is no such thing as a correct version of what happened. Our memories are what we are. I can't deny what any of us regard as the truth, and we can't deny our mother's. One thing I do know.

"I will never forget today. I will never forget what Sean just told us. We may all remember different words but we each will recall that something happened today that changed our world. It was not our mother's funeral, and it had nothing to do with the past."

Even as she said the words, Sophia knew, and she saw the others knew, that she was wrong. How each person remembered what had happened and what had been revealed on that day had everything to do with the past.

Lightning Source UK Ltd.
Milton Keynes UK
19 December 2009

147770UK00001B/6/P